Ready for anything.

The way Kendall had shoved her fingers into her shiny curls when she said that shouldn't be the least bit sexy. But Cheyenne loved playing with a woman's hair, especially when they didn't have any styling gunk in it. Hers would feel amazing.

He wasn't crazy about the taste of makeup, either. If he kissed Kendall, she wouldn't taste of makeup. Or smell like hairspray. She'd smell like sugar cookies. He wouldn't have to worry about getting lipstick on his shirt, or... whoa! How the hell had the topic of kissing her popped into his head?

He slid his window all the way down and took a long, slow breath.

"Cheyenne, are you okay?"

"Just fine."

"Your breathing was unsteady and I thought maybe you were feeling lightheaded from hunger."

"No, ma'am."

"Then it's time to talk about what I'd like you to do for me."

STOKING THE COWBOY'S FIRE

ROWDY RANCH

Vicki Lewis Thompson

Ocean Dance Press

STOKING THE COWBOY'S FIRE
© 2022 Vicki Lewis Thompson

ISBN: 978-1-63803-949-5

Ocean Dance Press LLC
PO Box 69901
Oro Valley, AZ 85737

Visit the author's website at
VickiLewisThompson.com

1

"I have a proposition for you, bro." Cheyenne McLintock slid onto a barstool near the cash register where his twin Clint was reconciling the receipts. Only a few Fluffy Buffalo customers remained and the band was packing up.

Clint held up one finger and kept working.

"Want a beer while you wait?" Their little brother Rance wandered down from the other end of the polished antique bar, a towel flung over one shoulder. "It'll have to be on the house since he's closing out the register, but—"

"Thanks, anyway." Considering the favor he was about to ask, mooching a beer wasn't classy.

"Just as well." Rance flipped the towel off his shoulder and began polishing the bar. "He just gave me the side-eye for offering. But shoot, one beer, y'know? It's not so much. The markup is—"

"Cool it, Rance," Clint muttered as he closed the drawer on the vintage cash register with a clang and tipped his head toward the remaining customers.

"Oh. They're so quiet I kinda forgot they were still here. Sorry."

Clint heaved a sigh and shook his head. "Fortunately for you, my boss has gone home for the night. If she'd heard you say that in front of customers, she would've fired you on the spot."

"It's not like they don't know we make a profit."

"Of course they do, but it isn't your place to remind them. You gotta start thinking before you start working your jaw."

"And I will, I promise. I love bartending here. The way I see it, eventually you'll move onto bigger things and I'll take over as manager."

Cheyenne snorted. "In other words, he's gunning for your job."

"Too bad for him that I'm very happy right where I am." He leaned his forearms on the bar. "What's this about a proposition?"

"Take my place tomorrow night." Cheyenne kept his voice low. "I'll make it worth your while."

Clint's eyebrows rose. "In the first place, it wouldn't work, and besides—"

"It would work. All you need is a haircut. And a shave before the event."

"And then what? Whoever has the winning bid gets you as their errand boy for seven days. Even if I fooled everybody at the auction..." His attention shifted to the customers as chairs scraped. "Thanks, folks! Have a nice night!" He gave them a tip of his hat.

"We'll do that, Clint," one of the guys called out. "Hey, Cheyenne, thank you for your service, son."

"You're welcome, sir."

"Guess we'll be seeing you up on stage tomorrow night."

"Yes, sir." His gut tightened. He'd rather face a wall of flames with a leaky fire hose.

"As I was saying." Clint made eye contact. "It's not just the auction. There's—"

"It is just the auction. Then we'll switch again and I'll take care of the hired hand aspect. I just don't want to go up on stage and strut around. That's not me."

"I know that, but sometimes you have to take one for the team. I'll bet the rest of the guys aren't all that eager to—"

"Are you kidding? They think it's a hoot. We'll be doing this gig bare-chested, wearing only our turnout pants and boots, like you see in those firefighter calendars. They've been practicing their walk, like they were on a runway or something."

"And you're not practicing?"

"Oh, yeah, I'm practicing. I want them to think I'm gonna do it. But I've had this Plan B in my head for weeks. That's why I've let my hair grow out a little more. It's still not quite the same length as yours, though, so you need a trim."

"If you've planned this for weeks, how come you didn't ask me a long time ago instead of waiting until we're twenty-four hours away?" He glanced at the digital clock mounted under the bar. "Less than twenty-four."

"I kept thinking I'd get used to the idea. Instead I hate it more than ever. Today I finally faced the truth. I need you to switch with me. It's the only answer."

"But you work with these guys. Some of them for years. They'll know right away I'm not you."

"Not if they don't expect it. They'll be jacked up on adrenaline, ready for their five minutes of fame. I asked to be last, the grand finale, so to speak, so you can come in late. That way you don't have to hang around with them before you go on."

"Clint, you should stand in for him." Rance thumbed back his hat. "They need that new engine. You'll be way better than he will, which means you'll raise more money."

"See? Rance gets it. I don't have the showmanship to bring in the big bucks. You do. You'll be helping me and the community at the same time."

"Isn't Mom going to be at this auction? She'll bid you up."

"That's exactly what I don't want. She could end up winning me, which would be stupid. She's already the station's biggest donor. The other day she told me if the auction doesn't produce enough for the engine, she'll make up the difference."

"I see your point."

"C'mon. We used to switch places all the time."

"Yeah, when we were younger. When it was funny to confuse people. But these days I'm more me. And you're more you."

"Folks still mix us up."

Clint gazed at him, clearly searching for a different solution. "What if I coach you? Let's put on your music and do a run-through."

"When?"

"Now. Perfect opportunity. Nobody's here."

"Hey." Rance flipped the towel in Clint's direction. "I'm here."

"A run-through in an empty room won't bother me. It's the public humiliation I'm trying to avoid. And the excellent chance I won't earn a dime for the cause."

"I'll be the audience." Rance grinned. "I'm great at publicly humiliating people."

"Y'know, a coaching session could work." Clint flipped a switch behind the bar and the speakers hissed.

"No, it won't. Just take the gig for me."

"I'm sure you're not as bad as you think. What's your music? I've got most everything here."

"Strip It Down, but I—"

His twin laughed. "That Luke Bryan tune? Did you pick it, bro? 'Cause that's a very sexy—"

"I did *not* pick it, but the guys said if I was going last I had to have that one, which is why I want you to—"

"Cue it up, Clint." Rance vaulted the bar, one of his favorite show-off tricks, and grabbed a seat at a front table. "I'm ready to be en-ter-*tained*."

Clint fiddled with the sound system. "There it is." He glanced up. "Seriously, this impersonation thing could easily go south. Let me give you a few tips on your routine and you'll be fine."

"Aw, hell, I don't—"

"Show me whatcha got. Then we'll talk."

"Okay. I guess that's the only way I'll convince you." Turning, he walked over to the steps next to the bandstand. "Roll it!"

As the piano intro to the song began, he climbed the steps and sashayed across the stage. He liked the song, turned up the volume anytime it came on the radio in his truck, but walking around a stage to that slow-burn rhythm... no, thank you.

"Give us a smile, cowboy!" Rance called out in falsetto.

He turned and flashed a cheesy grin at his little brother.

"Rotate your hips," Clint said.

"While I'm walking?" He stopped and stared at Clint. "How're you supposed to do that?"

"I'll show you." He hopped up on the stage. "Rance, go start the music again."

"On it, boss. Need to fetch my phone, anyway."

Good Lord. "Rance McLintock, if you shoot a video of this, you're a dead man."

"Would I do that?"

"I mean it, little brother. I'll take a hammer to that phone if I see it pointed in my direction."

"You're no fun."

"So I've been told."

"First off, start out like this." Clint took his position at the edge of the stage as Rance rebooted the tune. "Swivel your hips as you come toward center stage, like so." He demonstrated the move. "Then pause and do a hip rotation in the middle."

"Ooooo, baby, you are *so* hot!"

Rance's high-pitched imitation of a groupie made Cheyenne laugh.

Clint did, too, but he kept his sexy movements going. "Exactly! You gotta have fun with it. Laugh, smile, loosen up." He stepped back. "You try it."

"Here goes nothing." He walked to the far side and attempted Clint's swivel-hipped stroll toward center stage.

"Ooooo, baby, you look soooo constipated!"

Clint cracked up. "Sorry." He took out a bandana, wiped his eyes and cleared his throat. "But he's right."

"Told you."

"I thought maybe if I showed you, you'd be able to—"

"Not in a million years. Switch places with me?"

"Yes. Yes, I will." He looked over at Rance. "Didja get it?"

Rance held up his phone and grinned. "Best blackmail material ever."

Leaping from the stage, Cheyenne stormed toward his little brother. "Dammit, I warned you not to—"

"Just messing with you, bro." He handed over his phone. "The video's just for you. Thought you'd get a kick out of it. Then you can delete it."

"Wait." Clint jumped down and came over. "Let me look at it before you erase it."

Holding the phone out so they could all see, Cheyenne hit play. By the end of the video he was laughing so hard he couldn't talk. His brothers were in the same shape, red-faced and gasping.

Clint was the first to catch his breath. "Classic. Please don't get rid of it."

"I'm not gonna." He forwarded the video to his phone and deleted it from Rance's. "But I want sole possession."

2

On the day of the bachelor auction, Kendall Abbott developed a case of jitters. She hadn't had an attack of nerves this bad since the championship round of Montana's annual spelling bee.

Thank goodness her best friend Angie McLintock had suggested an afternoon ride with lots of cross-country galloping. Good weather added to her excellent plan. Although snow still topped the Sapphire Mountain range, new grass poked through the brown crust that remained from last summer's forage.

Spring. A season of beginnings. In the past she'd observed the change more than she'd participated in it, but not tonight. Walking the horses back to cool them down gave her a chance to talk bachelor auction strategy with Angie.

Loosening Mischief's reins, she let the bay gelding choose his own pace. "Who do you figure my competition will be?"

"Hard to say." Angie pulled her dark hair into a ponytail and anchored it with her baseball cap. "How long's it been since he broke up with what's-her-name from Missoula?"

"It was sometime before February twenty-third."

"How do you know that?"

"I asked about her when I finally got him to come over and inspect your wiring job in my kitchen. He said it hadn't worked out."

"I'm not surprised. High maintenance."

"No kidding. I saw them at the Buffalo one night. She went into the bathroom to fix her hair and makeup at least ten times."

Angie laughed. "Not that you were counting."

"Didn't have to. I was with Lucky and he started keeping track."

"That's my brother, all right. A detail guy."

"Yeah, he's funny."

"You two get along great. Have you ever wondered if—"

"We decided to kiss one time, to see what happened. Nothing. It just made us laugh."

"For all you know, that would happen with Cheyenne, too."

"Oh, something would happen, all right. I get goosebumps just thinking about him."

"Then why haven't you just laid one on him?"

"He always stays out of range. But if he's obligated to spend a bunch of time with me, my odds are better."

"The clerk over at the Baby Barn might bid on him."

"Adele?"

"Yep. I went in to pick up something for Beau and Jess's baby shower and he was there for the same reason. Adele was falling all over herself. Customer service with a capital C."

"Was he flirting back?"

"Nope."

"That's good. I doubt she has deep pockets, anyway. Anybody else who might want him?"

"That new server at the Chuck Wagon. She waited on Mom and me the other day and she brought up the auction. She asked us if Cheyenne is seeing anyone."

"She's cute, but she doesn't strike me as someone loaded with cash, either. It all comes down to the money. Unless someone shows up with a wheelbarrow full, he's mine."

"How high are you prepared to go?"

"As high as I have to."

"Whew. I'm glad this is Wagon Train we're talking about."

"Me, too. Your mom is probably the wealthiest resident. She won't bid against me."

"She won't once you throw out your first bid. I haven't told her you're doing this, but maybe I should. She plans to start the bidding high so he'll bring in more."

"That's fine. I want to support the fire department so I don't care how much I end up spending."

Angie peered at her. "I don't know how well-off your dad left you, but—"

"Your mom hasn't told you anything?"

"Like what?"

"A couple of months after Dad died, she came over to gently inquire if I needed any financial assistance. I showed her the books and she was relieved. Dad was a savvy investor and he taught me to be one, too."

"That's awesome. How come you never told me?"

"You never asked. I figured your mom had said something."

"She wouldn't. She respects your privacy."

"That's cool, but I don't mind sharing that stuff with you, if you're interested."

"I am now that I have a handywoman business and I'm responsible for my own retirement."

"We could trade investment tips."

Angie grinned. "I'm all over that idea. Between you and Mom, I'll be a financial wizard."

"Which reminds me. Are you laying out some cash tonight?"

"Nope. I've already made a private donation."

"Angie."

"It's easier on everyone if I date out-of-town guys."

"But—"

"My brothers wouldn't deliberately be threatening. But there's nine of them. They're an imposing bunch. Any potential boyfriend would think twice."

"A true hero would stand up to them."

Angie laughed. "I'm still looking for someone with the cojones to do that. Mom says that will be my litmus test. But back to you. I'm convinced you'll win Cheyenne tonight. What's your game plan?"

"That's just it. I don't have one. I can assign him plenty of jobs around my place during the day, but dreaming up reasons for him to stick around at night is tougher."

"He could take you dancing at the Buffalo."

"What if he treats me like his little sister, even at the Buffalo? We have dinner, dance a little, and he'll bring me home. End of story."

"You could invite him in."

"For what?"

"Isn't it obvious? Cheyenne's not stupid."

"He's also not motivated to be alone with me, let alone make a move. I'm cute little Kendall, his baby sister's best friend. In his mind I'm way too young for him even though I'm twenty-five and he's barely thirty. It's not my fault I look young for my age. How do I turn that around?"

"You could bake him sugar cookies. He's a sucker for those."

"I tried that when I had him over to do the fire safety check. He ate a couple and seemed to like them, but he still kept his distance."

"Are you sure you don't want to try a little makeup? This time I could—"

"It's no good, Angie. That makeover we did last summer was painful for my self-image. After you left, I couldn't scrub it off fast enough."

"It made you look older."

"So he'll take older me to bed and wake up to find younger me fixing breakfast? He'd freak."

"Maybe not. Especially if you're wearing the sexy nightgown you bought last summer."

"While I'm whipping up scrambled eggs and flipping bacon?"

"Why not?"

"I'd feel like an idiot. You don't cook in flimsy outfits. Things spatter. And that nightgown is still in a drawer, by the way. I've never worn it."

"Keep it handy. Makeup and slinky negligees work on guys. It arouses their lizard brain."

"Lizard brain? I want nothing to do with *that,* thank you very much."

"Oh, yes, you do. Tap into it and you have a chance of making whoopee with my big brother."

"I vaguely remember something about this. What does it control besides sex?"

"Basic stuff. Fight or flight, feeding, you get the idea."

"I fed him sugar cookies. Nothing happened."

"That doesn't mean he was unaffected. Mix those cookies in with other primitive instincts, and you could hit pay dirt."

"I never looked at it that way." She glanced down the trail to the fork about fifty yards away. The left fork led to Rowdy Ranch and the right would take her to the A-Plus, her parents' name for their small spread. "That's good info. I'll have just enough time to make cookies."

"Want to reconsider the makeup and negligee?"

"Not yet. Maybe I can appeal to his primitive instincts without those things."

"How?"

"I haven't worked out the details, but it might involve chickens."

"Your chickens?"

"Yes, ma'am." She drew back on the reins as they reached the fork in the path. "Are you still picking me up at six-thirty?"

"That should net us a front table. But Kendall... chickens? I don't get it." Angie looked flummoxed.

"It might work. Even if it doesn't, it'll be hilarious."

* * *

Kendall and Angie snagged the last front table at the Buffalo. Soon after they arrived and ordered drinks and snacks, Wagon Trainers had filled the rest of the seats.

Kendall glanced over her shoulder. "I've ID'd your brothers, sprinkled throughout the crowd like you said."

"Sky decided it was better than bunching up. They'll have more influence by creating pockets of energy. Mom's book club is doing the same."

"Lots of energy in here, for sure. The place is packed."

"I think it's because we've never had a bachelor auction in Wagon Train. And we have some great-looking firefighters."

"Do tell." Kendall gave her a nudge. "Any in particular you—"

"I'm not answering that."

"Aha! Which means you—"

"Oh, here comes Mom. Looks like she'll just make it. We need another chair. I'll go grab one." She located an extra one at another table and moved it to their two-top. "I should probably get her a drink from the bar, too. It's almost time to start."

Kendall smiled. "Nice diversionary tactics, girlfriend. They won't work on me."

Angie made a face and hurried off.

Desiree slowly wound her way through the crowd, stopping to greet people along the way, her copper curls shining in the glow from the antique lanterns hanging from the ceiling beams.

"I ordered us some more munchies." Angie returned with her mom's drink. "She needs to get a move on. I'll bet they're waiting for her to sit." She beckoned to her mother.

Desiree gave her a wave and maneuvered quickly through the remaining tables. "Good evening, ladies!" Taking off her coat, she draped it over her chair and sat. "Kendall, are you bidding tonight?"

"Yes, ma'am."

"Cheyenne?"

She flushed. "Yes, ma'am."

"Gonna get that boy?"

"Yes, ma'am."

"Excellent. Hey, I'm just in time."

The band played *Hail to the Chief* as Tyra Lindquist and Chief Denny Portman took the stage. Tyra introduced Denny and praised the dedicated crew of Wagon Train Fire and Rescue. Before turning the mic over to Denny, she announced that fifty percent of the night's food and drink proceeds would be donated to the station.

Desiree nodded in approval. "Classy move. I can see why Clint likes working for her."

"I heard the bachelor auction was her idea," Angie said.

"Then I'm doubly impressed. I'll write her a thank you note."

"So will I," Kendall said. And maybe, if the time spent with Cheyenne turned out well, she'd send the Buffalo's owner a bottle of champagne.

Chief Denny didn't waste any time getting the event rolling. Turning to the band, he gave a signal and they launched into Kane Brown's *Lose It*. The first bare-chested firefighter vaulted onto the stage and began to dance.

Kendall clapped and cheered as the evening continued at the same high pitch. Each bachelor was introduced with a different sexy song, followed by a spirited round of bidding. She also kept an eye on her friend, but Angie never gave herself away, darn it. Every bachelor received the same enthusiastic response. No favorites.

Cheyenne was last on the program. Would he play to the crowd the way the others had? That didn't fit his personality. He was reserved, a trait she was drawn to. Maybe he'd rise to the occasion, but this kind of event wasn't his style.

The bidding on the next-to-last firefighter ended and the band's keyboardist played the opening chords of *Strip It Down*. Evidently the quiet cowboy she'd known all her life would parade across the stage with this hot tune as his background. Disbelief warred with eager anticipation.

The fire chief stepped to the mic. "Ladies and gents, give it up for Cheyenne McLintock!"

He danced up the steps and crossed the stage, adding sexy moves that made her heart pound. The crowd whooped and hollered as he paused to execute a suggestive hip rotation.

Her mouth went dry. She'd been a Cheyenne watcher for years and he'd never acted like this. Was it because of the adrenaline rush, or because... *it wasn't him.*

She clapped a hand over her mouth to smother a giggle. He'd switched with Clint. A glance at her tablemates confirmed it. They'd ducked their heads and snatched up their napkins to cover their laughter.

Desiree was the first to risk looking at Kendall. Her eyes sparkled and she had to clear her throat before she could speak. "Still gonna bet?"

"Oh, yes, ma'am. We're perfect for each other."

Her eyes widened. "You and Clint?"

"Oh, no. Me and the cowboy waiting in the wings. He did exactly what I would have done."

3

Cheyenne stayed out of sight during Clint's performance. He didn't need to see it. The whistles and cat calls told him his twin was rocking the house. Perfect.

His mom threw out the first bid, although she had a tough time because she was so busy laughing. Rance had promised not to tell, but his family would catch on immediately.

Clint's sexy moves inspired several women to jump into the fray. His mom dropped out after the first round, but four others stayed in. He could only identify one voice for sure. Kendall. He sighed.

Angie had mentioned bringing her, but he'd convinced himself she wasn't bold enough to participate. Sure, she'd had a crush on him for a while, but he'd never given her an ounce of encouragement. In fact, he'd done everything possible to discourage her.

She might not be a teenager anymore, but that's what he saw when he looked at her. Unless he'd missed something, she'd never had a serious boyfriend. That could mean she was still a virgin.

She was totally wrong for a thirty-year-old cowboy who'd lost his virginity at seventeen. Clearly she didn't understand that.

Either her stubbornness or Clint's performance had lit a fire under her, because she wasn't backing off. The bids increased rapidly, shooting past the amount his buddies had brought in. One-by-one, she knocked out the competition until she was the last one standing.

The chief pounded the nail into his coffin. "Going once, going twice, sold to Kendall Abbott for a very nice sum! That puts us over the top, folks. Now we can afford that new engine!"

Thunderous applause greeted that announcement. He was glad for it, too, but holy hell. He'd be at Kendall's beck and call for a total of one hundred and sixty-eight uncomfortable hours. It would be like baby-sitting his little sister, except not anything like that because Kendall acted like she wanted him to kiss her. Which he was never, ever gonna do.

After the crowd settled down, Clint addressed Kendall from the stage. "Congratulations, Miss Abbott, and thank you for your generosity. Let me change clothes and I'll be out to join you so we can make plans."

Slipping into Clint's office, Cheyenne slumped in the office chair and waited for his brother.

Clint came in grinning. "Damn, that was fun!"

Vacating the chair, Cheyenne pumped energy into his response. "I'm glad. You were the right McLintock twin to handle it. I owe you one."

"Nah." He toed off the boots. "You don't owe me anything. I enjoyed myself. Your buddies from the station figured it out, by the way. So did Chief Denny. None of them cared. They knew you were dreading this." He stepped out of the turnout pants. "Good fit."

"Should be. Unless you've gotten fat in your old age."

"Not a chance. Tyra keeps me so busy I don't have time to get fat." He glanced at the pants and boots. "I can keep this stuff until tomorrow. You don't want to be lugging it when you have your chat with Kendall."

"Guess not."

Laying the turnout pants over the back of his chair, Clint pulled his jeans from the pile of clothes he'd left on his desk. "You okay? You seemed a little down when I first came in."

"Just thinking how I'll navigate spending so much time with Kendall."

"Ah." He zipped his jeans. "Worried that she'll get you in a hammerlock and take advantage of you?"

"Very funny."

"It's Kendall, bro. You've known her since she was splashing around in a wading pool with Angie, Rance and Lucky."

"That's the point. She's supposed to think of me like her big brother. Instead she's got this crazy idea we should be a couple. That's just wrong."

"So treat her like your kid sister, like you always do. She'll get over it."

"I'm not so sure. She just spent a small fortune for a sizeable chunk of my time."

Clint chuckled. "Blame that part on me." He buttoned his shirt and tucked it into his jeans. "She thinks you're hot."

"Smartass."

"How you talk. After I just saved your bacon."

"Sorry. You're right. It's not your fault if Kendall wants me even more, now."

"I was kidding about that. She knew all along who I was."

"She did?"

"Oh, yeah. She was sitting with Mom and Angie. Two seconds into my routine, they were all in hysterics. I was made."

"Then her bidding had nothing to do with your routine?"

"That's right." Clint picked up his hat, settled it on his head and tugged on the brim. "I'm pretty sure she enjoyed it, but clearly she came into the Buffalo with a game plan. Our switcheroo didn't matter to her. She was going to make the winning bid or else."

"That's very bad news."

"Look at it this way. Her determination to beat out the competition juiced the bidding. The station will get a new engine."

"That's the bottom line, isn't it? That's why the department staged this in the first place." He held out his hand. "Thank you."

"Anytime." Clint gripped his hand and pulled him into a quick hug. "You've got this. It's just Kendall."

"Right." He left the office ahead of Clint, who'd somehow convinced Tyra earlier that excessive paperwork had prevented him from attending the auction. Or could be Tyra was onto them, too.

Maybe the whole damn town had figured it out. Didn't matter. The event had raised the necessary amount to purchase a much-needed apparatus for the fire department. He hadn't participated in the auction, so the least he could do was honor the commitment to Kendall in exchange for her sizable contribution.

He put on his happy face as he approached the table. "Have a good time?"

His mom laughed. "It was like the old days."

"Except Clint and I didn't fool anybody at this table." He glanced at Kendall. "Thanks for putting us over the top."

"My pleasure." She flashed him a smile.

She had dimples. Of course she did. He'd seen them a million times. But tonight they caught his attention, for some stupid reason. "We should talk about what you want me to do."

"Absolutely."

Dimples again. Why was he so focused on them? "But we don't have to discuss it now. I have the next forty-eight hours off. I could come by in the morning and we could—"

"Or you could drive me home and we could talk about it on the way."

"Um, I suppose that would work." He shot a look at his sister, who was having way too much fun with this. "If you want, we could stay a while. Maybe you'd like some pie."

"Thanks, but I've been snacking all evening. I'm ready to go if you are."

"Then let's make tracks." He helped her out of her chair, took the coat that was draped over it and held it so she could put her arms in.

"Thank you, Cheyenne."

"You're welcome." This routine was way too cozy, too much touching, like they were dating or something. He'd never helped her on with her coat. She smelled like sugar cookies. Had she always smelled like that?

No. Either she'd been baking this afternoon or she'd dabbed on sugar-cookie perfume before she came here. Either way, he wouldn't fall for it.

He said goodnight to his mom and sister, who could barely contain their glee. If Angie was behind this bachelor auction move on Kendall's part, he'd have words with his beloved sister tomorrow.

Usually when he escorted a lady out of the Buffalo, he kept a hand at the small of her back. He almost made contact before he overrode his ingrained habit. Instead he just followed her out.

The wooden buffalo at the door moaned *haaaappy traaaaiiils toooo yooouuu* as they exited the building. Clint had refused to reveal how the sensors worked, but they were accurate enough to tell the difference between someone entering and leaving. Damned ingenious.

"Someday I'm going to figure out where the sensors are." Kendall stepped out on the sidewalk and turned to him. "Or do you already know?"

"No, ma'am. Clint's a vault. None of us can get him to crack."

"But now Rance is working there."

"And we thought he'd spill the beans the first week. But he hasn't. Whatever Clint threatened him with, it worked."

"Do you at least know who's the voice of the buffalo?"

"Afraid not." He gestured toward their right. "I'm down that way."

"I know. Angie and I drove by your truck when we were looking for a spot."

"My mom didn't drive in with you?"

"She had an important conference call with someone in California and had to come separately."

"I see." A studio had optioned one of his mom's books, but her bestselling career as Western writer M.R. Morrison was a secret. Even Kendall didn't know. The world thought the author was a man and his mom and her publisher wanted to keep it that way.

The vehicle that had parked next to him was gone, so he had plenty of room to help her into his truck.

Her hand was tiny and warm, but she had the grip of a lumberjack. "Thanks."

"You're welcome." When she finally turned him loose, he resisted the urge to shake his hand to restore the circulation. Closing the door, he rounded the hood of his truck and climbed behind the wheel.

"You keep your truck nice."

"Thank you." He started the engine and the radio came on. He switched it off. Something romantic might come on. Or worse yet, *Strip It Down.* But music could forestall conversation. He switched it on again. Except they needed to set up a schedule and now was as good a time as any. He turned it off.

"Is something wrong with your radio?"

"No. Why?" He checked his mirrors and backed out of the parking space.

"I thought you might have a loose connection since you kept switching it on and off. Sometimes that helps."

"Sometimes." He had a loose connection, all right. In his brain. That sugar-cookie smell filled the cab of his truck. He'd never considered sugar cookies as an aphrodisiac, but his libido seemed to think it was. Inappropriate urges regarding the person in the passenger seat had him breaking out in a cold sweat.

He needed to get rid of that arousing scent. The night was too chilly to put the windows down. But not if he ran the heater.

He flipped the heater switch and warmth poured from the vents. Then he lowered his window and breathed in a lungful of fresh air. He could still smell sugar cookies, but a cool breeze brought down his internal temperature.

"Why'd you do that?"

"What?"

"Turn on the heater and put your window down. That makes no sense."

"I'm partial to riding with a window down, but I didn't want you to get cold."

"I have a coat. You can turn the heater off."

"Okay, if you say so."

"I'll put my window down, too. The night air is bracing."

"Aren't you worried that your hair will blow?"

"Nope. That's why I keep it short. If you let curly hair get long, it's too much trouble. Angie has to spend a lot of time on hers."

"We're all aware of that."

"I keep telling her to cut it short like mine. All I have to do is wash it, run my fingers through it like this, and I'm ready for anything."

Ready for anything. The way she'd shoved her fingers into her shiny curls when she said that shouldn't be the least bit sexy. But he loved playing with a woman's hair, especially when they didn't have any styling gunk in it. Hers would feel amazing.

He wasn't crazy about the taste of makeup, either. If he kissed Kendall, she wouldn't taste of makeup. Or smell like hairspray. She'd smell like sugar cookies. He wouldn't have to worry about getting lipstick on his shirt, or... whoa! How the hell had the topic of kissing her popped into his head?

He slid his window all the way down and took a long, slow breath.

"Cheyenne, are you okay?"

"Just fine."

"Did you have any dinner tonight?"

"Yes, I did."

"I'm glad to hear it. Your breathing was unsteady and I thought maybe you were feeling lightheaded from hunger."

"No, ma'am."

"Then it's time to talk about what I'd like you to do for me."

Dammit, it was just a simple sentence. He didn't need to read anything into it. "Like what?"

"I checked with Chief Denny before you came to our table, and he said you were off-duty from now through Sunday morning."

"Yes, ma'am." His voice was a little raspy. He cleared his throat. "That's correct."

"Well, good, because I'd like you to spend the night."

4

Cheyenne's shocked expression was pretty funny, but he almost drove off the road. That would be a bad beginning for their first night together. Kendall shouted a warning and he corrected course just in time to avoid landing them in a ditch.

He gulped. "What do you mean *spend the night*? Are you suggesting we—"

"I'm hoping you'll stay up and guard my chickens." She managed to say it with a straight face.

"Chickens? You don't have any—"

"I just got them a week ago. Angie and I built the chicken coop and put up the fence. This morning I found evidence of some critter trying to tunnel underneath."

"Have you thought about getting a dog?"

"Yes, but I'd need to decide which dog and then train them. It's not a short-term solution."

"True. In the meantime, you could install a motion detector and—"

"Maybe, but I've reinforced the enclosure, and I'd like to see whether what I did worked. I'd also like to find out what is after them."

"Is that why you bid on me? To guard your chickens tonight?"

"Sort of." *And because you're flat-out delicious.* "I might need you to do it for two nights, just to make sure everything's okay. I'd guard them myself, but I'd fall asleep out there. Considering your career, I'll bet you're able to stay up all night." She hadn't meant that to have a double meaning, but it made her giggle inside.

"I hate to break it to you, but I'm not that good at staying up."

Yeah, he didn't get the joke. "Are you sure?"

"Ask the rest of the crew. They'll verify it."

Or laugh themselves silly. "You don't stay awake when you're on duty?"

"We sleep so we'll be well-rested when a call comes in. I'm the first to conk out."

"Then I guess there's only one solution. I'll stay out there with you."

"You know, on second thought, I can manage alone. You don't have to—"

"I think I do." Oh, yes, this was a much better idea. "We'll keep each other awake." She'd planned to bring him sugar cookies and coffee while he took on the manly protector role, but staying with him the entire night was a vast improvement on her original concept.

"If I'd known about this sooner, I could have rigged up that motion sensor for you."

"This literally just happened. I wasn't sure what I was going to do about it, but then I thought of asking you to keep watch."

"I could install a sensor tomorrow. First thing, I'll go to Miller's."

"What if my reinforcement job works? A couple of nights' surveillance will tell us whether it does or not. I might not need to buy anything."

"Well, it's your money, but I think a motion sensor in a chicken coop is a good investment in any case."

"But is it, really? When it warms up, I'll have bats flying around. They could trip the sensor several times a night. And I'd be hopping out of bed every time they do."

"I suppose." He drove in silence for a few moments. "Why'd you get chickens in the first place?"

"I like fresh eggs."

"So do I. But this is Wagon Train. A passel of folks keep chickens and sell eggs."

"Buying them from someone isn't the same as going out in the morning and collecting fresh-laid eggs for your breakfast. My dad talked about it and never got the chickens. So I have."

His cheek dented as he smiled. "Can't argue with that."

That smile was worth every penny she'd shelled out tonight. It gave her hope that a small crack had developed in the armor of resistance Cheyenne had worn ever since she'd come of age.

Her view of his strong profile in the light from the dash also justified her considerable investment. For years she'd yearned to be alone with him in the dark and she'd accomplished that much, at least. "So you're willing to guard the chicken coop?"

"Yes, ma'am. You paid good money for me at the auction."

"That doesn't give me the right to make you do something you'd rather not."

He chuckled. "I can tell you've never had a hired hand."

"How can you tell?"

"You're lousy at giving orders." He glanced at her, a teasing sparkle in his eyes. "You could have simply told me that you need that chicken coop guarded tonight. And I'd have replied *yes, ma'am*, and that would have been that."

"Isn't that what I said?"

"Afraid not. It was *I'm hoping you'll stay up and guard my chickens.* Which leaves the situation tentative and wide open for me to question the program."

"I see what you mean. But you're not a hired hand."

"That's exactly what I am. You've bought a week's worth of my time. You're allowed to tell me what to do, and unless it's dangerous, immoral or illegal, I'll do it."

That left a wagonload of possibilities. "Good to know."

"Where would you like me to park?"

"Right next to my truck is fine."

He shut off the motor and opened his door. "We should check out the coop first thing, in case they've been here while you were gone." Opening the console, he took out a flashlight.

Uh-oh. She had no idea when the intruders had arrived last night. "I sure hope they didn't." For a whole bunch of reasons. She opened her door.

"Wait, I'll get your—"

"Never mind. Follow me." If they'd been here and failed to get in, that tilted her all-night guarding plan over into ridiculous territory. If they'd been here and gotten in... she didn't want to think about it.

"How many chickens?"

"Three. Dolly, Loretta and Reba. Dolly has yellow feathers, Loretta has dark ones and Reba's are reddish. They're such pretty chickens. I hope they're okay." She rounded the side of the house and sighed in relief. A bright moon revealed a peaceful scene. No feathers.

Unless something had hauled them away, feathers and all. Yikes. "Could you shine your flashlight around, please?"

"Sure. Where's the point of entry?"

"There." She pointed to the spot. "You can't really see it anymore since I dug a trench around the whole fence and added another layer of chicken wire buried about eighteen inches deep. I had some railroad ties, so I shoved them up against the fence, too."

He gazed at her. "You did all that today?"

"It was important. Let's go around to the gate. I want to make sure the coop's still locked."

"The chickens are locked in?"

"Of course! I can't have them running loose if something's out to get them." She led him to the other side, shoved away the railroad tie with her boot and went in through the gate. "The lock's fine."

"I should hope so." He followed her in. "I haven't met any four-legged varmints who've learned to pick locks."

She glanced at him. "I suppose you're wondering why I want you to stand guard all night since I've put in double wire and railroad ties."

"It's crossed my mind." He surveyed the area. "This is the Fort Knox of chicken coops."

"Not necessarily. Something has discovered I have three tasty chickens in that coop. A coyote could leap the fence."

"And pick the lock?"

"No, but they're smart. They might find a way in that I haven't thought of."

"But you said the critter tried to dig under the fence."

"Right, which could still be coyotes, or a fox, badger, skunk or raccoon. If I can find out what it is, and how they're trying to get in, I can figure out the best defense."

"And that's where I come in."

"That's where *we* come in. Now that you've explained that you're not a night owl, we'll be working as a team."

"I'm not really sure how—"

"Trust me. I've got this. My back porch has a perfect view of the chicken yard. C'mon, I'll show you." She secured the gate and led the way to her back porch. "And we'll be armed with my night-vision binoculars."

"When did you get those?"

"Years ago just because I thought they were cool."

"I got some, too. Then I passed them down the line after the thrill wore off."

"Mine have been tucked away for ages. I'm glad I kept them, though." She climbed the steps. "As I said, perfect line of sight to the coop. And there's a nice glider for us to sit on."

"Ah."

"The metal seat was too hard and cold, so I added that thick seat cushion and some pillows. It's comfy."

"So I see." He swallowed.

"Tell you what. You can station yourself on the glider and keep watch while I fetch the binoculars and fix us a snack."

"Thanks, but I'm not really hungry."

"Then maybe you'd like something to drink. How about hot coffee?"

"Yes, ma'am. Sounds good. Black, please."

"Are you sure you don't want a treat to go with your coffee? I made cookies."

"Sugar cookies?"

"How'd you know?"

"Just guessed. You made them once when I was here."

Good, he'd remembered. Angie might be onto something. "I'll bring out a plate of them. You might get hungry. I'll bring a blanket, too, in case we start to get cold." She was counting on it.

5

After Kendall went through the back door, Cheyenne took stock of the glider. Obviously she intended for them to sit on it. Together. He'd do no such thing. Not in his current state.

He could have handled mucking out stalls, digging post holes, or checking out her fence line. He'd resigned himself to spending hours at her place. Daylight hours.

In bright sunshine, she looked like a fresh-faced teenager who'd never been kissed. Or at least not kissed the way he presently had the urge to do it.

At night, her eyes reflected the soft light of the moon. Her moist lips did, too. When she'd gotten wound up about the potential danger to her chickens, she'd taken quick little breaths. Parted her lips. Driven him crazy.

He'd damned near kissed that sexy mouth. Jamming his hands in his coat pockets and focusing on his surroundings had kept him from doing it.

But his body still hummed with awareness. The combination of her sugar-cookie scent and her short, sassy hair that begged for the thrust of his fingers had him tied up in knots.

If she had a critter nosing around her chicken pen, he prayed that animal would make an appearance soon. Once they'd identified the culprit and come up with a logical deterrent, he'd cut and run.

Why was she suddenly so tempting? She was his sister's best friend, and likely a virgin to boot, which put her firmly in the "no touching" zone. Then why the hell was that the only thing he could think about doing?

"Coffee's almost done. I brought you the binoculars so you can scan the tree line." She came out with the binoculars, two mugs and a folded blanket tucked under her arm.

He moved toward her. "Let me help you with that."

"Just take the binoculars." She handed them over. "I've got the rest." Setting the mugs on a small table in front of the glider, she laid the blanket on one end of the seat. "Go ahead and sit. I'll be out in a jiffy."

"Thanks, but I can see better if I stand."

She paused, her tantalizing mouth pursed. "I get that. But it could end up being a long night. You'll probably want to take some breaks."

Not on your life. "We'll see how it goes."

She gave him a slow smile. "Yes, we will." Then she turned and sashayed into the house with a decided sway to her slim hips.

His breath caught. What the hell? Where'd she learn a seductive move like that? Probably on

TV. She was lucky that she was trying out those moves on a guy who wouldn't take unfair advantage of an inexperienced woman.

Clearly she was in the mood to cuddle under that blanket, maybe even make out a little. But a randy cowboy with minimal control could look at this setup and assume she was ready to rock and roll.

Yeah, good thing he was the one she'd brought home tonight. She'd grown up with him and his brothers and might think all men were like the McLintocks. Not by a long sight. Maybe he'd mention that before he left.

"Seen anything yet?" She came out the door balancing a plate of cookies in one hand and holding a thermos in the other.

"Not yet." Hadn't been looking, either. That hip action of hers had made him forget his job. He took the cookies and set them next to the coffee mugs. "I'll make another pass."

"Ready for me to pour your coffee?"

"Yes, please." Nudging back his hat, he adjusted the binoculars and studied the shadows along the tree line located about seventy-five yards from the house. Then he checked around the chicken pen. "All's quiet."

"Then you can certainly spare five minutes to sit and drink your coffee."

He turned around. "I don't..." Her hopeful expression weakened his resolve. What was so wrong with sitting on the glider with her? She wasn't likely to pounce on him. And she'd made cookies.

Besides, he couldn't be on the lookout for a varmint and canoodle at the same time. If she cozied up to him, he had a legitimate reason to reject her advances, one that shouldn't hurt her feelings.

She'd moved the blanket to her lap, which allowed them each more room. Because she was slim, he could sit without his hip brushing hers. He set the binoculars on the table and settled down close to the arm rest, but not so close he'd look paranoid. "Those cookies smell fresh."

"I baked them before I left for the auction." She leaned over to pick up her coffee and a cookie.

He waited until she'd moved back before he reached for his coffee and a cookie. Taking one was the polite gesture, since she'd made the effort. And his mouth needed something to do. "Guess you know these are my favorite."

"After all these years being your neighbor? Of course. Seemed like the least I could do when I was asking you to give up sleep for the sake of my chickens."

"Maybe we'll get lucky and the critter will show up sooner rather than later." He bit into the cookie. Oh, man, that was good. He took his time chewing and swallowing. "Is that my mom's recipe?"

"Sure is. I pester her and Marybeth for recipes all the time. It must be great to have two experienced cooks at the ranch."

"More like two experienced moms. I was so young when Marybeth and Buck came to live with us that I can't remember a time they weren't there."

"They're very sweet. Marybeth taught me to braid my own hair. And she supervised the first time I made her chicken soup to make sure I got it right. I was twelve."

"You've been cooking since you were twelve?" He took another bite out of that soft, sweet cookie. If he kissed her now, she'd taste just like it. But he wouldn't be doing that, would he? He devoured the rest of the cookie and reached for a second one.

"Long before that. Dad tried, but his heart wasn't in it. I've always liked making food. And growing it. I have seedlings in pots ready to go out when it gets warm enough."

"I admire your grit." He reached for a third cookie. So delicious. "It's a short growing season."

"Good soil helps. I've been working on mine and it's much better than when I started."

"How's that?" Soil was a safe topic. Especially if he kept his hands and mouth busy with cookies.

"For the past few summers I've fed it lots of organic matter to make it more robust. It's been so responsive to that."

"Ah." Maybe not so safe. She'd managed to make dirt sound sexy. And the cookie plate was almost empty. "Then you've had good harvests?"

"I have, but I love planting even more. There's nothing like sliding my fingers into the warm earth and feeling the rich moistness there. I get such satisfaction from planting my seedlings."

Was she saying stuff like that on purpose? Nah, no way. She'd blush if she could read his mind. Her description of fondling the earth was precisely how he wanted to fondle her. As for planting seedlings... that was forbidden territory.

Much more of this conversation and he'd have an obvious problem. He'd need that blanket on his lap instead of hers. Standing, he grabbed the binoculars from the table. "Better check out the tree line. See if anything's moving." Other than his pride and joy, ha, ha.

"While you do that, I'll refill the cookie plate." The glider squeaked as she stood.

He should tell her that he'd had enough cookies. It was the God's truth. He'd lost count of how many he'd scarfed up while she'd carried on about fingers sliding into warm earth.

But if she kept the discussion going along those lines, he'd need that plate refilled. Someone should warn her not to talk like that if she didn't want to be ravished within an inch of her life. And who better than him to inform her of the risk she was taking?

Except he'd have to reveal that her unintentionally suggestive comments had affected him. He didn't want her to know that. But if he didn't admit that she'd aroused him, why would she believe his claim that her innocent words could lead to unexpected consequences?

"See anything out there?"

"Still looking." Once again, he'd stood on her porch staring into the distance while he wrestled with his libido. And his pride. Raising the binoculars, he surveyed the tree line. Nothing.

Then he trained them on the chicken pen. "Kendall." He kept his voice low. "Something's out there."

"There is?" She hurried over to stand close to him.

Very close. He handed her the binoculars and stepped away from her warmth. "By the gate. Looks like a fox. But a very small one."

"I see it," she murmured.

That soft murmur sent a message straight to his privates.

"It's not a baby, though." She sucked in a breath. "What if it's a swift fox?"

"Here? That would be highly—"

"I know, but look for yourself." She returned the binoculars. "We can't see the colors, but the markings are right."

He forced himself to focus on the issue at hand. "It looks like pictures I've seen. It's circling the pen, looking for an easy way inside."

"It won't find one. And it's too small to jump the fence. Is your phone camera good enough to get a picture? Mine's too old and cranky."

"It has a low-light feature. I'll try." He gave her the binoculars, pulled out his phone and quickly changed the setting. "Maybe if I zoom in...whoops, it's leaving." He snapped as many shots as he could as the fox trotted away. "That's it. Out of sight."

"Come over to the glider. Let's see what you've got."

He choked back a laugh. She hadn't meant it that way. Once they'd settled on the glider, he clicked on the string of pictures he'd taken. "They're grainy, but it's possible a wildlife expert could confirm whether we have a swift fox in the neighborhood."

"Wouldn't that be exciting?" She scooted closer. "Aren't they endangered?"

"They were. Might still be. I haven't kept up with it. Whether they are or not, the population I read about was in Canada with a few straying down to northern Montana. But not here, that's for sure."

"You can't always predict what animals will do."

"Or people." She was so close, caught up in the excitement of spotting a rare species, her sweet body pressed against his. If he was the kind of guy to capitalize on the moment... but he had a conscience, a moral code, and a little sister who was Kendall's best friend.

Turning off his phone, he edged away from her. "Looks like you found your potential intruder."

"A tiny fox, who might be far away from his or her pack. And not strong enough to dig through my double wire fence. He could be more vulnerable than my chickens."

"Right."

"Tomorrow we need to contact people and find out what we should do, who needs to know about this sighting."

"Good idea. Listen, Kendall, I—"

"You're going home, aren't you?"

Putting down his phone, he turned to her. "Yes, but first there's something I need to tell you before I leave."

She eyed him warily. "Okay."

He took her by the shoulders. Probably a bad idea, but the contact steadied him. "Ever since we left the Buffalo, I've been fighting the urge to kiss you."

"You have?"

"I don't think you realize how appealing you are and how your innocent little remarks could give someone the wrong idea."

She burst out laughing, startling him. "What about the right idea? What if I desperately want you to kiss me and everything I've done tonight is toward that end?"

He blinked. "Everything?"

"All of it. Asking you to protect my chickens, baking you your favorite cookies, letting you know I love making food and growing—"

"Even the sexy words about digging in the dirt?"

"Yes, damn it! I'm trying to appeal to your lizard brain."

"My *what?*"

"You know, the primitive part that's focused on food, sex, and—"

"Good grief. You've been talking to Angie."

"She told me about the lizard brain thing. She thought I should put on some makeup, but I hate makeup so I dreamed up these other tactics."

She was adorable and he was seconds away from losing control. He released her and put some distance between them. "Evidently you don't need makeup to access my lizard brain."

"Then I succeeded?"

"You did."

"Hallelujah! Then let's—"

"But you've bitten off more than you can chew."

"I have not!"

He softened his tone. "Yes, you have. Tell me the truth. Are you a virgin?"

"What if I am?"

He sighed. And searched for the right words. "You don't need a guy like me. You need... someone who's more your speed."

"A twenty-five-year-old virgin?"

The horror in her voice made him grin. He liked her. A lot. "Okay, maybe a twenty-six-year-old guy with some experience."

"What if I want a thirty-year-old cowboy who's been around the block?"

"You just think you do. The reality—"

"Wait, let me get this straight. You just admitted that I turned you on tonight."

"Yes, ma'am."

"Then I have to conclude the idea of taking me to bed wouldn't be your worst nightmare."

"No, but that doesn't mean—"

"I want you to take me to bed, Cheyenne. Not tonight, not after we've talked it to death. But tomorrow night would be fabulous."

"You don't know that."

"Yes, I do. Listen, here's how I want to play this. Go home, get a good night's sleep. Come back in the morning. I'll have plenty of chores lined up. We'll contact folks about the swift fox. We'll spend the day together. And then... we'll see."

He smiled. Couldn't help it. Finding out she'd tempted him had given her cojones. "Now that's how you talk to a hired hand." Standing, he tipped his hat. "See you first thing in the morning, boss."

He left the porch fast, because if he didn't, he was going to do something he'd deeply regret. She was way too charming and he needed to shore up his defenses. He'd have better luck with that in the light of day.

6

Cheyenne wanted her. Kendall couldn't fall asleep and didn't care. His words ran through her head on a loop she could listen to all night. Victory!

Eventually her pulse rate settled and she drifted off, hours later than she usually did. The rumble of a powerful engine and the thud of a truck door closing brought her immediately awake.

He was back! He'd changed his mind about waiting until tomorrow night! Leaping out of bed, she ran barefoot to the front door and flung it open. Cold! So cold! She grabbed her coat from the hook by the door and pulled it around her shoulders.

"Morning, boss!" He gave her a smile as he climbed the steps to the front porch.

"Morning?" Gasping for breath, she peered over his broad shoulders to the rim of light gilding the horizon.

"Looks like somebody slept in." He approached slowly, his gaze moving to her granny gown.

"I…um…yes." She glanced down at the material, white flannel dotted with pink flowers. "If

I hadn't announced my virginal status, this nightgown would have."

"Your nightgown talks?"

She looked up and caught the teasing gleam in his eyes. "If it did, it wouldn't have much to say."

"I'm not so sure. It's privy to secrets no one else knows." The light in his eyes shifted from teasing to something much warmer.

She forgot to breathe. "Would you... like to come in?"

"No thank you, ma'am." He took a step back. "Just need to know where you want me to start."

She sighed. "I should have put on my slinky nightgown just in case something like this happened."

"You have a slinky nightgown?"

"Angie talked me into it when we went shopping last summer, the same day she gave me a makeover. I've never worn it. I should have put it on before I answered the door. Then you'd have come in."

"Not true."

"Just now you were looking at me as if you were considering it."

"Because I was."

"If I'd put on the slinky nightgown, that would have pushed you over the edge."

He chuckled. "My lizard brain would have made me do it?"

"Probably. But now we'll never know because I came out in my virginal granny gown."

"To tell the truth, that granny gown has my lizard brain doing backflips."

"I don't believe you."

"You mean because I'm standing out here instead of rolling around with you on your bed?"

The air left her lungs and she could only nod as a blast of heat made her loosen her grip on the coat.

"I'm as susceptible as the next guy to that kind of primitive urge. But I was raised to be a gentleman. We all were. That means my lizard brain doesn't get to be in control of my actions."

"Oh."

"Your feet must be freezing."

"Nothing on me is freezing right now."

"That makes two of us."

She swallowed. "I won't think less of you if you decide to come in."

"I'll think less of myself. You told me last night how you want the day to go and it's a good plan. We need to spend time together and think this through. Talk some more."

"Why? I've known you all my life."

"Not the way you want to know me, now."

Another flood of heat through her system left her shaky. "Guess not."

"What needs doing first? The horses or the chickens?"

Me. "The horses, please. I'll take care of the chickens."

"If you'll tell me where the chicken feed is and how much you give 'em, I'll do that, too."

"I have a certain routine and I'd like to keep it the same. I'll throw on some clothes and handle the chickens."

"Alrighty, then. I'll be in the barn if you need me." Touching two fingers to the brim of his hat, he turned and clattered down the steps.

I need you. He claimed to have mastered his primitive sexual urges. She couldn't say the same.

How could she? Hers had only surfaced seconds ago when he'd calmly mentioned rolling around in her bed. He wasn't some girlish fantasy. He was real. And he made her ache like the fantasy never had.

He was determined to follow a sensible schedule — ranch chores, friendly conversation, civilized behavior. She didn't have time for that. The schedule needed to change.

Dashing back to her bedroom, she was dressed and had her coat on in no time. Egg basket in hand, she hurried out the back way to the chicken pen. Good thing the little fox wasn't an immediate threat.

But she needed to ramp up her protection plan in case a bigger threat came along. Not today, though. Tomorrow, when Cheyenne was on duty at the firehouse, was soon enough. She didn't want to waste a single minute of this day. Or night.

"Good morning, ladies!" She moved the railroad tie and opened the gate. "Time for breakfast!"

Rustling and clucking noises from inside the coop made her smile. They were eager for their food, no question, but they likely appreciated the delivery routine, too.

Closing the gate behind her, she set down the basket, pulled a key from her pocket and unlocked the door to the coop. Then she opened it and began singing Dolly Parton's *Here You Come Again*.

Dolly strutted out in perfect time to the song. Reba followed, bobbing her red-feathered head to the catchy rhythm. Loretta, the shy one, ventured cautiously down the wooden ramp. Not a dancer. But with more time, maybe she'd get there.

Kendall kept the tune going as she flipped the catch on a metal bin, filled a large scoop with seed and two-stepped in a circle, scattering a ring of it around her. The song was the perfect length, and she gave it a big finish as she tossed out the last of the seed.

"No wonder you didn't let me feed the chickens. I can't carry a tune in a bucket."

She glanced up. Cheyenne stood just outside the fence, hands in the pockets of his shearling coat. His warm smile sent moisture rushing to her lady parts. "I think they like it."

"So do I."

"Are Mischief and Mayhem all set?"

"Munching on their hay. I left them to it so I could find out what you'd like me to take care of while they're eating."

"Funny you should mention that." He took her breath away, but she had just enough air in her lungs to get the words out. "I do need you to fix something for me."

"What's that?"

"Come on in the house and I'll show you."

"Sure thing." He opened the gate for her. "You keep the barn so ship-shape, I'll have trouble finding things to do in there once I muck out the stalls."

"That's okay." She led the way to the house. She didn't dare look at him. "I expect this issue to take quite a bit of your time. It's something I really can't do by myself."

"Then I'm glad I'm here to help. Must be electrical or plumbing."

"Electrical." She was so turned on her ears were buzzing. Electrical, right?

"Seriously? I just inspected everything in February."

Not everything, cowboy. "It just started."

"When?"

"This morning."

"Wow. Lucky I'm here to check out the problem."

"Very lucky." She climbed the back steps.

Quickening his pace, he made it to the door ahead of her and opened it, gesturing her inside.

"Thanks." She whisked past him, her heart pounding. Breathing had become a problem. Would she pass out from lack of oxygen? That would be inconvenient. She barreled through the kitchen.

Behind her, the click of his boot heels picked up speed. "You didn't say it was urgent. Is this an issue that could cause a fire?"

"Sure is." She hurried into her bedroom and spun to face him.

"Whoa, there." He pulled up short to avoid running into her. "Show me the problem."

"Right here. It's me." She gulped for air. "If you don't make love to me this minute, I'm gonna go up in flames."

7

"*Now*?" His brain stalled. The rest of him raced full speed ahead. "We need more time." *He* needed more time. Didn't he? "We have to sort out the implications of—"

"I'll never make it the whole day." Breathing fast, she tossed her coat aside and reached for the hem of her pink sweatshirt.

"Wait!" He made a grab for her but she scooted out of reach. "Don't take off that—"

"I'm not kidding, Cheyenne." She whipped the sweatshirt over her head, dropped it on the floor and reached behind her back for the catch on her bra.

And he watched, because he was human. Since his body had bypassed his useless brain, it was busy sending heated blood south and a shot of adrenaline to his heart, giving him the shakes. "But I thought—"

Her plain cotton bra landed on the pile of clothes at her feet. Her perfect breasts trembled as she toed off her boots. "When you said that about rolling around on my bed, you tripped a switch."

He swallowed. And she'd just tripped his. Could he override it? "This is your first time. It should be special."

"It will be. You're here."

"It shouldn't be me."

"Don't you understand? I *want* it to be you. Ever since our talk on the front porch, I've had this intense craving, this ache deep inside. I honestly can't stand it. Please. Take off your clothes."

"I don't have a condom."

"I do."

"*You*? Why?"

"Because the bachelor auction was my big chance and I knew you wouldn't have any." She shoved off her jeans and panties. Her socks came with them.

He sucked in a breath, stunned by the delicious view of a naked Kendall. Her sweet breasts would exactly fit his cupped hands. He could easily span her narrow waist, pick her up and... yeah, he was toast.

She glanced at him. "What?"

"You're... so pretty."

"Thanks." She walked around the end of the four-poster, giving him a view of her enticing backside. "That was nice of you to say, but now I need you to—"

"I wasn't being nice. You're beautiful."

"I'm glad you think so." She climbed into the unmade bed, but instead of getting under the covers, or even lying down, she sat upright and stared at him. "I hope my body helps you make the decision."

"Heaven help me, it does." He took off his coat.

"Goodie."

"This is definitely a mistake." Unfastening his cuffs with unsteady fingers, he unbuttoned his shirt halfway and pulled both shirt and T-shirt over his head. "But it looks like I'm going to make it."

"It won't be a mistake. If you want to keep it a secret, I will."

"Even from Angie?" He held onto the footboard so he could yank off his boots.

"Yes."

"Thank you."

"What if I hadn't had condoms? Would you have vamoosed?"

"With you sitting there looking so eager? No, ma'am. But I would have had to do things differently."

"That would be nice, too. Maybe for the next go-round, after we have coffee."

One of her earlier comments penetrated the red haze fogging his brain. *I expect this issue to take quite a bit of your time.* "You want to spend the day in bed?"

"Yes."

"How can you even decide that when you've never—"

"Do the ladies you've been with enjoy themselves?"

"I make sure they do."

"Then why wouldn't I want to stay in bed with you all day?"

"Because you're not in shape for it. Sex uses different muscles. Too much friction might make you—"

"Cheyenne! Stop talking about friction and get undressed so you can provide me with some!"

"Yes, ma'am." He unbuckled his belt, unbuttoned his jeans and unzipped.

"Friction is the whole point. Let me decide if it's too..." Her voice trailed off.

He stepped out of his jeans and took off his briefs. "Is something wrong?"

"Oh, no." Her voice was breathy, almost a whisper as she gazed at his cock. "I'm just having a moment."

Her expectations were beginning to intimidate the hell out of him. "You know, the first time, it might not be as wonderful as you're imagining."

"Or it could be twice as wonderful." She continued to stare at his manly attributes.

"Sometimes your body has to learn how to have orgasms."

"It already knows."

"Oh?" Maybe she wasn't quite so innocent. He walked to the other side of the bed. "You've experimented?"

"I tried a battery boyfriend, but it wasn't my style. I decided to hold out for the real deal."

"I see." All he had to do was deliver the amazing experience she'd been anticipating ever since puberty. And do it better than some gizmo with various settings and hours of battery life. No pressure. He stood beside the bed, gathering his forces. "Where's the condom?"

"I have more than one." She pointed to the nightstand beside him. "They're in that drawer."

He opened it. So many condoms. And his brand. In fact, the brand all his brothers used. Somebody had told her. Somebody named Angie.

His little sister's fingerprints were all over this situation. The chances of her not finding out what went on here today were zero. But he was past the point of no return.

Pulling a foil packet out of the drawer, he laid it on the nightstand.

"You're not going to put it on?"

"Not yet." Despite the intensity of the moment, he smiled. She might want him to climb on board ASAP, but he had a laundry list of things he wanted to do before that happened.

"But I told you I need—"

"Please indulge me. Slapping on a condom and diving straight into the main event isn't my preference, especially when you've never done this before and we're new to each other."

"Oh."

He slid back the covers, scooted onto the wear-softened sheets and mimicked her position, sitting hip to naked hip. The heat from her body nearly torpedoed his plan. He took a breath and refocused. "We haven't even kissed."

"I figured we'd get to that."

"Let's get to it now." Wrapping an arm around her shoulders, he coaxed her to make a half-turn in his direction. He mirrored the move and tunneled his fingers through her silken curls. "You have great hair."

"I do?"

"Been thinking about it for hours." He combed through it as the glow in her eyes intensified. "Been thinking about this, too." Tightening his grip, he lowered his mouth to hers. His heart pounded as he made contact. *Easy. Easy.*

Her velvet lips parted, inviting him in. He fought the impulse to plunge deep. Skating on the razor edge of his control, he thrust gently with his tongue.

With a soft whimper, she clutched the back of his head and slackened her jaw. With a groan, he took more, and more yet. Pressing her down to the pillow, he cupped her breast.

When she gasped, he drew back. "Too much?"

"There is no such thing." She'd never used that sultry tone before. "I want it all." Sliding her hand down his chest, she wrapped her fingers around his cock.

He swallowed a groan and resisted the urge to grab that condom. He gazed into gray eyes darkened with passion. "What do you think you're doing?"

"Trying to get you to ravish me." She gave him a squeeze.

He gulped.

"Is it working?"

"Damn it, Kendall, this is supposed to take more than five minutes. Once I put on that condom—"

"I'll be in paradise! I loved how you kissed me. I want a whole lot more of that. But I also want this." One more squeeze, with a little more force.

His balls tightened. "Watch it, you'll make me come."

"Because you're as worked up as I am?"

"Yes."

"Then do it. For both our sakes."

He threw up the white flag. "You win." He reached for the packet on the bedside table.

"We both win."

"There's that." He tore it open with his teeth and rolled on the condom one-handed Evidently extreme lust increased motor skills. "Since you keep begging me to do this, I assume you're ready." But he slipped a hand between her thighs to make sure.

When he touched her there, her breath caught. "I'm beyond ready."

"I do believe you are." Moving into position, he leaned down and brushed his mouth over hers. "After this, you won't be a virgin anymore."

She wrapped her arms around his back. "I can't wait."

Lifting his head, he focused on the luminous gleam in her eyes. "Then here goes." He pushed partway in.

Her eyes widened.

"You okay?"

She nodded. "More, please."

"Yes, ma'am." He buried his cock in her warmth and squeezed his eyes shut. *Don't come don't come don't come.* He fought off the orgasm with everything he had. She felt so good. Too good. He was in big trouble.

8

Flooded with pleasure, Kendall didn't dare move. Or even breathe. What if she was dreaming that Cheyenne was naked in her bed with his amazing cock deep inside her?

The sensation of having this beautiful man locked in tight, his heaving chest brushing hers, surpassed every other special moment in her life. Total bliss.

Except Cheyenne didn't look at all happy about it. Eyes squeezed shut, his breath coming in quick gasps, he was clearly in agony.

She took the risk of waking up from this excellent dream. "What's wrong?" She stroked his very warm, very tense back.

His eyes slowly opened. "Huh?"

"What's wrong? You look like you're in pain."

His lips twitched. "I'm not."

"They why do you look so miserable?" His ragged laughter created an interesting vibration in her core.

"I'm the opposite of miserable. I'm in heaven."

"But your face was all scrunched up."

"I was working hard not to come. Took some effort." He smiled. "I'm better, now."

"I didn't mean to make you work hard. I want you to have a good time. You could have—"

"I would never have forgiven myself. The guy you asked to be your first finishes in three seconds? I'd have to turn in my man card."

She stroked his bare back some more. Because she finally could. And his muscles felt even better than they'd looked under his shirt. "No one would ever know."

"I would. You've waited years for this experience. You deserve the best I have to give."

She'd waited years for *him.* But saying that might freak him out. "Thank you."

He chuckled. "Oh, you're welcome." Leaning closer, he dropped light kisses on her cheeks. "Happy to help."

She closed her eyes. "That feels nice."

"I'm glad." He eased his cock back and slid in again. "How about that?"

"Makes me tingly down there."

"Good tingly or bad tingly?"

She looked up to find him watching her. "Definitely good."

"Then let's try some of that friction you asked for." Holding her gaze, he set an easy pace. "You can move with me, if you want. Just lift your hips when I—yeah, perfect." His breathing changed. "Nice."

"Mm, I like this." She tightened her grip on his back. "I get a jolt of feeling when we come together."

"That's the idea." His voice roughened. "Let's speed it up." He pumped faster. "Good?"

"Uh-huh." The first spasm startled her. "Oh!"

"That's promising."

"Very... ahhh, *Cheyenne*....

"I'm here. Let go. I've got you."

She gasped as her body clenched again, and then... the dam broke. Arching upward with a sharp cry, she held on, trembling from the force of her climax. He kept thrusting, wringing more cries from her as the waves of pleasure washed over her again and again and again....

With a deep groan of surrender, he drove in one last time. His body tensed, then shuddered as he swore softly and gasped for air.

She held him close and smiled. He'd never said some of those words in front of her before. Maybe he didn't think she could hear him. She almost couldn't, as loud as her heart was beating.

Dragging in a breath, he looked down at her. "You pack a wallop, lady."

"Is that why you were swearing?"

"You heard that? I'm sorry."

"Don't be sorry. If you were swearing because I pack a wallop, then it's a compliment."

"I was and you do."

Reaching up, she cupped his face. "So do you. That was the best."

He smiled. "Not much of a contest, since it was your first, but I'm glad you liked it. I can do better."

"I can't imagine anything better. Didn't you hear me shouting for joy?"

"I did." He gave her a sweet kiss. "And I'm glad you had a good time. But as they say, you ain't seen nuthin' yet." He eased away from her and got out of bed. "Be back in a minute."

She sat up. "Does that mean you're in favor of staying in bed all day?"

"Yes, ma'am," he said over his shoulder as he headed for the attached bathroom.

"Woo-hoo!" Throwing both hands in the air, she did a little lap dance in the bed.

"But we can't forget about Mischief and Mayhem. They need to be turned out and their stalls cleaned," he called through the open door.

"If we do it together, it'll go twice as fast."

"It will, unless we get distracted."

"Why would be get distracted?"

"We'll be working side-by-side. Now we know what it feels like to be naked together. That can be distracting."

Excitement stirred in the very place he'd recently visited. "You mean do it in the barn?"

"It's been known to happen. And it's not like you have anyone around to take notice of what we do."

"I've never been naked anywhere but in my bedroom and my bathroom."

"Are you saying you're too shy to consider such a thing?" He walked out of the bathroom in all his naked glory.

Her blood run hot and moisture collect in all her significant places, including her mouth. She swallowed. "The barn sounds great. Right here, right now sounds even better."

His manly attributes responded. Fascinating. The first time he'd been fully aroused when he'd taken off his jeans. Now the miracle was happening right before her eyes. "That's a gratifying reaction."

"I'm very grateful."

Her body began making demands, the same ones that had motivated her to lure him in here in the first place. "Let's do it again."

"Not so soon."

She gazed up at him. "I need you. And you want me. I can tell."

He chuckled. "No kidding."

"Just one more time. Then we'll go turn the horses out."

He stood looking at her, warmth in his eyes. "I can fix this. Sit on the side of the bed."

"Why?"

"I'll show you."

"Okay." She swung her legs over the side of the bed. "But it doesn't seem like we're heading in the right direction."

"I think you'll change your mind in a minute." He dropped to his knees in front of her.

"But you're way down there and I'm... oh, wait." Her insides began to quiver. "I get it."

Sinking lower, he hooked her legs over his shoulders. "Just a little something to tide you over."

"What about you?"

"Never mind about me. Just lie back and relax."

"*Relax*? I'm hopping like a jumping bean inside. Are you really going to—"

"Yes, ma'am."

"What if I don't taste good?"

"Oh, you will. Guaranteed. Lie back."

She flopped to her back, shivering with anticipation. "Go ahead."

His laughter sent a warm breeze over parts of her that were very damp. Then he swiped his tongue over one certain part and she came unglued, yelling out a very unladylike word.

"For the record, you taste delicious." He started licking.

And she began to pant. When he switched to a combo of licking and sucking, she pounded on the mattress with both fists. "I. Love. This."

He lifted his head. "Thought you would." Then he went to work in earnest.

She quickly lost her mind. When her first climax made her thrash around, he anchored her more securely with a firm grasp of her hips and gave her a second one.

As she lay breathless and limp, saturated with endorphins, he nuzzled his way back to her mouth. Then he pressed her gently into the mattress and gave her a deep kiss, sharing the flavor on his lips.

Abandoning her last shred of modesty, she clutched his head and reveled in the erotic taste. Her body hummed in the aftermath and he prolonged the buzz, massaging her sensitized breasts and stroking her trembling thighs.

At last he lifted his mouth from hers. "Better, now?"

"Am I glowing?"

"Maybe a little."

"I feel like I am. I've never... that was..." She trailed off with a sigh. "I can't find the right words."

"So you're happy."

"Happy doesn't begin to cover it."

"I'm glad."

"I've read about this, but naturally I've never... I'm *such* a fan."

"Then we have a good alternative?"

"I wouldn't say that."

"You wouldn't?"

"I loved it. But you didn't get to come."

"That's okay."

"I'm not an idiot. I could—"

"Later, maybe, after I've had a shower. First we have horses to deal with, and I'm pretty sure you've missed breakfast."

"Don't care, don't care, don't care."

He smiled. "All things considered, you might want to keep up your strength."

"Oh. Good point."

"I vote we eat breakfast, then turn out the horses and muck the stalls."

"You didn't have anything to eat, either?"

"Not much."

"Why? I didn't demand that you show up at a certain time. You didn't have to rush over here."

"True."

Her heart did the happy dance. "You grabbed something quick for breakfast and hopped in your truck." She grinned. "Tell the truth and shame the devil. You couldn't wait to see me again."

He met her gaze. "I told myself to slow down. I told myself that we were *not* going to end up in your bed tonight."

"And you stuck to that. We ended up here this morning."

"Yes, ma'am."

"Regrets?"

"No, ma'am." Sliding his arm under her shoulders, he lifted her to a sitting position and sat back on his heels. "But if we don't get moving, we'll be back there again."

"In other words, we need to pace ourselves."

"Exactly." He stood and walked over to his pile of discarded clothes.

"Give me time and I'll learn the ropes." She planted both feet on the braided rug by the bed and pushed upright. She was wobbly from those orgasms, but she'd get her sea legs in a minute. "I've never had a lover."

He turned, his jeans in one hand. "I didn't say it before, but I'm honored that you chose me to be your first."

Forever and always. "I had a hunch you'd be the right one."

9

Kendall hadn't been kidding about loving to cook. He didn't mind doing it, and he was willing to pitch in to help, but he didn't relish the process.

Evidently she did. Once she was in the kitchen, she began eagerly pulling out pans and utensils, her face alight, her happy smile showing off her dimples. What a bright spirit.

"This'll be fun." Then she paused. "We need more eggs."

He glanced at a small bowl of unwashed eggs on the counter. She'd done her research. Unwashed eggs didn't need refrigeration, which robbed them of flavor. "Isn't this enough?"

"Not if I'm making omelets." She started toward the back door.

"Yum." His stomach rumbled. "I'll come with you." He followed her, not that she needed help gathering the eggs. Her interaction with the chickens charmed the heck out of him, though, and he didn't want to miss that. "Gonna sing?"

"That would confuse them, since I'm not feeding them. I'll be sure to thank them for their efforts though."

"Good idea. You want happy hens." The sun warmed his back. No need for a coat anymore today.

"I want them to be happy. That's why Angie and I made the pen so big. When I can trust them not to run away, we'll go sit in the grass together."

"And do what?"

"We have story hour in the afternoon. Maybe not today, but tomorrow, when you're at work, I'll take a blanket out to the pen and read to them."

He chuckled. "Let me guess. *The Little Red Hen.*"

"Ha. Much as I love that story, I wanted something longer. I've started with M.R. Morrison's first book."

"Oh, have you?" His mom would be tickled that her book was entertaining Kendall's chickens.

"I read a bunch of them when I was in high school. I'd forgotten how good they are. Have you ever read him?"

"Some. Here, let me get the railroad tie for you." He moved it aside.

"Well, you should try some more. They're excellent. One of his books even has a main character named Cheyenne." She unlatched the gate. "Hello again, ladies! Bet you wonder why I left that basket behind."

The black-feathered one, Loretta, scurried away at her approach, but Dolly and Reba cocked their heads and fixed her with a beady-eyed stare.

"I was distracted by this handsome cowboy." She gestured in his direction. "You know how that goes." She crouched down and both chickens slowly approached, bobbing their heads and making soft clucking noises. She lowered her voice. "Just between us, he's great between the sheets."

He swallowed a laugh so he wouldn't startle the hens. "Thanks."

"You know you are."

"And now your chickens know. Or two of them do."

"They won't talk, will you, girls?" She ran a hand over the back of each one and they stayed put, as if they enjoyed it.

"Do they like to be stroked?"

"All ladies like to be stroked." She continued to gently pet the hens, who clearly were into it.

She was teasing him, and he had the resistance of a rabbit. At this rate they wouldn't make it through breakfast. "Did you come out here to talk about sex?"

She glanced back at him and her dimples flashed. "Didn't intend to. It's just where my mind is, I guess."

"I see that. I'd suggest we postpone those omelets, but then the whole program falls apart."

"Sorry, not sorry."

"Tell you what. You don't need me to collect those eggs, so why don't I turn Mischief and Mayhem out and meet you back in the kitchen?"

"Does that mean we won't have barn sex?"

He groaned softly. "I've created a monster."

"I'll behave. I want to make those omelets. I know how much you love them."

"Did Angie give you a list of my favorite foods?"

"She didn't have to. I've spent plenty of time hanging around with your family. You make no secret of what you like and don't like."

"That I do." But did she keep track of everybody's preferences? Likely not. And she finally had a chance to show off her knowledge. "See you in a few." He headed out of the pen, latched the gate and made tracks for the barn.

Had this day been inevitable? Could be, considering Kendall's determination and Angie's willingness to facilitate the episode. His little sis was usually wiser than he gave her credit for, something she reminded him of regularly. Maybe she knew what she was doing in this case, too.

Now that the deed was done, he was at peace with the outcome. No question he was a safe choice, maybe the safest one, for Kendall's first sexual adventure. He'd enjoy it while it lasted and be happy for her when she was ready to move on.

Mischief and Mayhem, both good-looking bays, were delighted to see him. Good thing he'd decided to let them out before having breakfast with Kendall. *Breakfast* could end up taking a while. Not that he minded.

Mischief was taller than his mother but otherwise the family resemblance was strong. Even his white blaze was similar to hers. Mayhem had been Kendall's dad's horse, at least officially. Rumor had it that he gave up riding when Kendall's mom died.

Props to Kendall for her sunny disposition despite having lost both parents. He'd been so busy avoiding her over the years, he hadn't taken the time to admire her for that.

He led the horses out to the pasture, where new grass was soaking up the May sunshine. Near as he could tell, both horses were sound, so Kendall must be keeping them in shape. Not easy when one person had two horses to exercise. He added another item to the growing list of things to admire about her.

Leaving Mayhem and her son to kick up their heels in the pasture, he replaced the lead ropes. The stalls needed mucking out, but that could wait. He could smell the bacon and coffee from here.

His stride lengthened and his appetite increased—for food and for Kendall. He'd never made love to a woman who refused to indulge in makeup, nail polish, fussy hairstyles or sexy nightwear.

He didn't have to worry about smearing her lipstick. Her eyelashes wouldn't come unglued and her hair was soft to the touch instead of stiff and unyielding. She was ready to tumble into bed at a moment's notice. That was damned appealing.

Taking the porch steps two at a time, he opened the kitchen door, eager for the sight of her.

She stood by the stove, his phone in her hand. "Somebody really wants to talk to you. They've called three times."

That couldn't be good. He deflated a little. "Let's see what they want." The messages were all from Chief Denny. Chances were good this lovely interlude was about to end.

He called back and the chief picked up.

"Glad to hear from you, Cheyenne. Ralph's got a case of food poisoning and we're down one. I called Tom, but his wife's out-of-town at a conference and he's with their kids. Stewart took his auction winner to a concert in Denver. You're all I've got."

"Yes, sir. I'm at Kendall Abbott's house taking care of a few things, so I'll need—"

"Just get here when you can."

"I'll be there within the hour."

"Thanks, Cheyenne. Appreciate it."

"Yes, sir." He disconnected and looked at Kendall. She looked as disappointed as he was. "A guy's out sick."

"Figured it was something like that. The omelets are done. Can you stay long enough to eat them?"

"I can do that. I'll shower at the station. Just need to wash up before I sit down."

"The sink's all yours." She stepped out of his way, opened a cupboard and took out a couple of plates. "I'm glad you're staying for breakfast. I couldn't eat both and I hate wasting eggs."

"The eggs and your effort." He rolled back his sleeves and soaped up. "Everything smells great." Especially her. Nothing like the scent of a woman who's been thoroughly loved.

"In case you can't tell, I adore cooking for friends." She dished up the omelets and added several strips of nicely browned bacon.

"I feel lucky to be one of them." He dried his hands on a towel hanging near the sink and turned toward the kitchen table in time to help her into her chair. "Looks terrific."

She smiled, showing off her dimples again. "Does it appeal to your lizard brain?"

"Yes, ma'am." He took his seat. "You've got that down to a science. Angie will be proud." Laying his napkin in his lap, he met her startled expression. "You can tell her."

"I can?" She paused with her fork in midair. "Really?"

Her delight made him laugh. "I appreciate your promise to keep quiet, but guaranteed somebody in the family will notice if I start spending my free nights over here. It'll come out."

"And that's what you'll be doing? Spending the night with me whenever you're not on duty?"

"It's an idea—"

"But if you're here all night and doing chores for me all day whenever you're off-duty, then I'll use up my week too fast. I'd rather have you skip the daytime shift."

Reaching over, he covered her hand with his. "We've moved way past the original agreement."

Her breath caught. "Meaning?"

"You're not going to use up your hours. This isn't about you buying my time anymore."

"What is it about?"

He hesitated. He likely was her training wheels, a safe entry into her sexual future. But he wouldn't say that now and maybe not ever. She might come to the realization on her own. "Let's leave that discussion for another time, okay? When I don't have to eat and run."

"Okay. I just have one question."

"Shoot."

"When will I see you again?"

"Ralph will likely volunteer to take the last part of my shift since I'm finishing up his. My best guess is I'll be off Monday morning. I'll let you know." He dived into his omelet. And immediately had a party going on in his mouth. He closed his eyes and hummed with pleasure.

"You like it?"

He chewed and swallowed. "Best omelet I've ever tasted."

She gasped. "Seriously? Better than Marybeth's?"

"Yes." He forked up another good-sized bite. "But if you tell her I'll deny saying it."

"My lips are sealed."

As he savored his omelet, bacon done just right and a mug of strong coffee, he glanced at those tempting lips that she claimed were sealed. If he had more time, they wouldn't stay sealed for long.

"You want to kiss me, don't you?"

He kept eating. "Mm-hm."

"I thought so. You had that look on your face."

He finished off the bite he'd just taken. "I'm wondering why you're watching my face instead of eating the delicious omelet you put so much time into. It's going to get cold."

"I don't care if it does. I won't set eyes on you for two days. I'll eat after you leave."

He held her gaze. "I'll miss you, too." Heaving a sigh, he jabbed his fork into the last bite of omelet. "I'm sorry I have to leave."

"Me, too, but the department needs you more than I do right now."

"Afraid so."

"Anyway, when you get off duty, just come over to the house and walk right in. The door will be open."

He continued chewing as he lifted his eyebrows.

"Want to know where I'll be?"

He nodded, although he had a hunch what was coming. Clearly his cock did, too.

"In bed, naked, waiting for you."

His jeans grew tight. Quickly swallowing that last bite, he pushed back his plate and stood. "Thanks for an incredible breakfast."

She got up, too. "Are you going to kiss me goodbye?"

"No, ma'am." He grabbed his coat and hat. "That would put me in danger."

"Of what?"

"Getting fired." He touched two fingers to the brim of his hat and skedaddled before his lizard brain took charge.

_**10**_

Despite having Cheyenne's blessing to tell Angie whatever she wanted to, Kendall postponed contacting her friend. She wanted to talk about it, was eager to get Angie's input, and yet....

Cheyenne's decision to shower at the firehouse indicated he'd go straight there. His family might assume he'd be with her today unless she called Angie and told her he wasn't. Solitude gave her a chance to relive potent memories of him while they were still fresh.

If she stayed put, she wouldn't have to wash his scent off her skin. She could take a nap in the afternoon and breathe in the musky fragrance of her sheets, thrilling evidence of her first-ever sexual encounter with a man.

And what a man! Every virgin deserved to be initiated by someone who balanced genuine passion with caring restraint. She was lucky, but then again, she'd picked Cheyenne to be her first a long time ago. She'd chosen well.

Usually she changed her sheets on Saturday, but she wouldn't be doing that. Leaving the bed exactly as it had been when they'd rolled around in it, she walked down to the barn.

She looked at that building with new eyes, now. It wasn't just for keeping horses anymore now that Cheyenne had suggested it as a place to fool around. She couldn't wait.

Fetching the wheelbarrow, a rake and a shovel, she mucked out both stalls and laid down fresh straw. What did Cheyenne have in mind when he'd suggested barn sex? A blanket on a bed of straw? Or a vertical maneuver up against the wall?

She'd watched that second scenario in the movies. Looked like a challenge, but with Cheyenne's muscles, he'd be up to it. Lordy, he had eye-popping... well, *everything.*

Now that she'd been treated to the full monty, would she ever be able to look at him without wanting to strip him naked? If they were with other folks, especially his *family*, for God's sake, would they be able to tell what she was thinking?

She'd check with Angie, who had more experience in that department. Angie might have some tricks for handling a constant state of lust. Or not, since she dated out-of-towners and didn't bring them to the ranch.

Maybe the urge to jump Cheyenne's bones would wear off, eventually. If so, she didn't want it to happen anytime soon. Being in the know and having a willing partner with a beautiful body and a kind heart was the coolest thing that had ever happened to her. She wanted it to last as long as possible.

Around five, Cheyenne texted her. *Told Angie yet?*

Not yet. Maybe tomorrow.
That's why my phone isn't lighting up.
How's work?
Quiet. Boring.
Boring is good.
So you say. I could use a distraction.
Miss me?

Yes, ma'am. Gotta go. I'm in charge of dinner.

Sleep tight.
You, too.

She didn't hear from him again. But when she fell into a deep sleep, she dreamed of their wedding day. She'd had the dream countless times, but it had always been a wispy vision without substance. Now it was earthy and real. Sexy. No doubt about it, Cheyenne wanted her. At last she had a fighting chance to make her dream come true.

But to increase the odds, she needed advice. Now that her dad was gone, she had three sources — Desiree, Marybeth and Angie. Fortunately she had easy access to all three. After she'd fed the horses and the chickens in the morning, she showered and texted Angie.

Her reply came right back. I'm up at the main house with the family. Marybeth made waffles for breakfast. We have oodles of yummy toppings. Come eat with us. You can have Cheyenne's share.

Kendall hadn't had waffles in ages. Her dad had loved them, but making them for herself had seemed silly. *I'll be there after I turn out Mischief and Mayhem.*

Waffles prepared by Marybeth in the retro kitchen at Rowdy Ranch and eaten with whatever members of the family had gathered was a treat not to be missed. She debated riding over, but taking her truck meant she could leave her jacket at home.

Beau and Jess arrived when she did. "Been bit by the waffle bug, I see." Beau called out as he helped Jess out of the truck.

"Couldn't resist." She waited for them at the foot of the porch steps. Six months into her pregnancy, Jess's baby bump now prompted smuggling-a-watermelon jokes. "How's little Maverick coming along?"

"Just fine." Jess laid a hand on her round belly. "She's executing high kicks worthy of a Vegas showgirl, usually at two in the morning. Me, I'm taking lots of naps."

Beau nodded. "Me, too. I'm a napping fool. Love 'em. If you ask me, we don't have nearly enough midday shuteye going on in this country."

Kendall laughed. "Why are you taking naps? You're not pregnant."

"For solidarity." Beau put one arm around Jess's shoulders and the other around Kendall's as he ushered them up the steps. "To show my support for Jess's need to nap."

"Don't believe a word of it, Kendall. His idea of a nap is way different from mine. I lie down to sleep. He lies down for something else entirely."

"It's not my fault. Pregnant ladies turn me on. Which means we're going to have lots of babies. Right, sweetheart?"

"I'll agree to nothing until after you've changed several dozen diapers, lover boy." Jess glanced over at Kendall. "Watch yourself with these McLintock boys. They have way too much charm for their own good."

"I'll keep that in mind." But she didn't need to worry. Cheyenne had just the right amount of charm.

McLintocks filled the Rowdy Ranch kitchen, milling around as Marybeth presided over the waffle iron, announcing each arrival of a toasted confection from the griddle.

"Two more ladies in the house," Sky called out. "Stand back, bros."

Kendall glanced at Jess, "You get the next one 'cause you're preggers."

"Thanks, I'll take it. I'm starving."

"Believe her," Beau said. "You don't want to get between Jess and the next waffle."

"He's exaggerating. But not by much." Jess took a plate and claimed her prize.

Kendall picked up a plate from the stack on the counter. Desiree's vintage Boots and Saddle dinnerware was collectible, but she used it with abandon. She was constantly hunting online to replace pieces that inevitably bit the dust.

The next waffle came out like all the others — golden brown and giving off a scent that made Kendall's mouth water. "Thank you, Marybeth. It's beautiful."

"You're welcome, sweetheart." Marybeth's gaze was full of curiosity.

But since the whole family was assembled, including Cheyenne's twin brother, finding a chance to satisfy Marybeth's curiosity and ask for advice would be tricky. Turning away from the waffle iron, she held up her plate. "Okay, I've been served. You boys can duke it out for who goes next."

"There will be *no* fighting over my waffles." Marybeth's commanding voice more than made up for her short stature. "Line up by birth order."

Kendall took her plate to the counter filled with delicious options, chose a combo of Marybeth's cherry and blueberry preserves and topped them with a dollop of whipped cream. Then she headed over to the corner where Angie stood with her mom and Penny.

Angie edged closer and lowered her voice. "Have a good time yesterday?"

"The best."

Angie's eyes widened. "Did you—"

"We did."

"*Awesome.* Can't wait to—"

"Marybeth, ma'am?""

"Yes, Rance?" Marybeth finished pouring the creamy batter into the waffle iron's grooves and closed the lid. The batter oozed out the sides as it expanded.

"Why do we always line up oldest to youngest?"

Angie grinned as she nudged Kendall. "I want to see how this plays out."

Marybeth turned toward Rance, her waffle fork poised in midair. "Because that's the fair way to do it."

"Seems like reversing it sometimes would be more fair."

"Not for me and Bret," Marsh said. "We'd still be in the middle."

"Okay, good point. Then we could draw numbers. I just—"

"Rance, honey." Marybeth fixed him with a stern glance. "You're cute as a bug in a rug, but you need to learn how the cow eats the cabbage."

"But—"

"When Sky and Beau came along, your mama was scraping by. Nobody was going to the movies and loading up at the snack bar, if you know what I mean."

"I do, but—"

"As things improved, she splurged a little more with each baby. When you and Lucky showed up, she had the funds to spoil you rotten, which she did." She turned back to the waffle iron and lifted the lid. "Sky, come fetch your waffle." She put it on his plate and filled the waffle iron with more batter.

"That makes sense," Rance said. "Except by that logic, Angie should be last."

Angie's startled *huh* made Kendall turn to her, eyebrows raised. Angie blinked and opened her mouth to speak. "I—"

"She can't be last," Lucky said. "She's a girl."

"You know what?" Carrying her plate, Angie walked over to Rance. "You're right. I shouldn't be treated differently. I'll line up after you guys from now on. I'd give you my waffle, but I've eaten almost half."

"And I'd take it except you probably put butter on it and I like mine with—"

"Rance." Sky gave him a blistering look. "A gentleman doesn't take a lady's waffle. You know better than—"

"Hang on, Sky." Angie laid a hand on his arm. "How many times have I complained that you guys are overprotective of me?"

He heaved a sigh. "A few."

"Meanwhile I've enjoyed my position as the little sister, taking my privileged spot behind Mom for all kinds of stuff. I can't have it both ways. Rance just made me see that."

"Well, I don't see it." Sky's chest puffed out a little. "It's like the lifeboat thing. Women and children first."

"But we're not on the *Titanic*. We're in line for waffles."

He rubbed the back of his neck. "I still don't like it."

"But it's fair, Sky."

"Anyway, Mom should be first, no matter what."

"Agreed."

"And Penny gets to go ahead of me."

"I can see that."

"Same for Jess." Beau put his arm around his wife. "I'll give her my seat on the lifeboat any day."

"Your gallantry toward your wives is lovely." Angie gazed at Sky and Beau. "But promise me you'll never think of me, Penny, Jess, or Mom, for that matter, as weak or incapable."

"Or me." Kendall spoke up. "And since I'm the same age as Rance and Lucky, I belong at the back of the line, too."

"Well...." Marybeth's brow furrowed. "Except you're—"

"She's right," Desiree said. "If Angie's moving to the back of the line, so should Kendall."

Kendall had loved that woman since her first visit to Rowdy Ranch, when Desiree had given her a ride on Angie's Shetland pony. But she'd never loved her more than now.

Guaranteed Marybeth had started to say she should be treated as a guest. Thanks to Desiree's intervention, she was now officially a member of the family.

_11_

The brush fire had been a nasty business, taking up the entire day, but it was finally out. The structures in its path—a small ranch house and a barn—had survived. Cheyenne enjoyed the rush of adrenaline from a job well done.

Another helping of the stew he'd made the night before would be welcome, along with some sleep. Maybe they wouldn't get a call tonight. Back at the station, he checked his messages. Holy hell. So many messages.

He read the one from Ralph, who'd texted that he'd recovered and would take over for him in the morning. Good news. He could go see Kendall in the morning. His groin tightened.

The slew of texts from his family could wait until he'd showered and grabbed some chow. Clearly Kendall had spilled the beans today.

But she hadn't texted him to say she had. Or to ask how his day was going. Or pop in with a smiley face. Nothing. He would have liked her to make some contact.

Not surprising that she'd be hesitant to contact him at work, though. Endearing, in a way.

She likely didn't want to bother him while he was busy fighting fires, protecting property and saving lives. His family had no such hesitation.

The crew enjoyed dinner around the battered table that was as old as the firehouse. When the chief had asked if they wanted a new one since they had extra funds, he'd been shouted down.

Today's fire had turned out well in the end, so jokes flew as they relived the highlights and lowlights of containing the blaze. Times like this reaffirmed why Cheyenne loved his job.

Once the meal was cleared and the dishes washed, guys headed for their bunks. Cheyenne threw on a jacket and picked up his phone. He needed to deal with the family fallout before he headed over to Kendall's house in the morning.

He walked out into the cool evening and gazed at the row of texts. Still nothing from Kendall. So he called her.

She picked up with a breathless *hi.*

"Hi, yourself. By the way, you can text me when I'm on duty. I might not be able to reply for a while, but usually I find time."

"That's good to know. Have you heard from Angie?"

He chuckled. "Among others."

"What others?"

"The usual. Mom. Angie. Marybeth. Clint. Sky. Rance. I think Bret and Gil had a craft fair today or I likely would have heard from them, too. Marsh and Lucky aren't as text-crazy as the others."

"There was a craft fair. Bret and Gil had to leave as soon as they finished their waffles."

"Ah, so Marybeth made waffles and they invited you over?"

"Correct."

"Did you make an announcement during breakfast? Is that why I have all these texts?"

"Of course not, silly. I wouldn't broadcast it to your entire family. I waited until after breakfast was over. Then I got the women aside."

"You only wanted them to know?"

"In a way, although I'm sure Penny tells Sky everything."

"That explains the text from Sky. But not why I got one from Clint. And Rance."

"They were still in the kitchen and they might have figured out what we were huddling about."

"I'm sure they did. What was the reaction when you told the ladies? Were they surprised?"

"Not really. I didn't expect them to be. I just confirmed that thanks to you, I'm no longer a virgin."

"You said it like that?" He would have preferred less specific wording.

"Why not? It's the truth. And I wanted to get everyone's advice since I'm new at having sex."

"Everyone?" A trickle of sweat ran down his spine.

"Absolutely. Especially your mom and Marybeth. They've been at this longer than Penny, Jess, or Angie."

He gulped. "You asked them for sex tips?"

"Brilliant, right?"

A sudden brain cramp kept words from coming out of his mouth.

"Cheyenne? Are you still there?"

He cleared his throat. "Yes, ma'am."

"Are you upset that I asked for their advice?"

"Not upset." She was so earnest and sweet. He didn't have the heart to tell her she'd freaked him out. But if she used the tips from his mom and Marybeth, he never *ever* wanted to know. "I'm just tired. We had a long day. A brush fire."

"Goodness! Are you okay? Is it out? Was anybody—"

"It's out and no structures burned. Everyone's fine."

"What a relief. I should have asked you first thing about what happened today."

"All's well that ends well. And Ralph's taking over my shift in the morning."

Her breath caught. "You'll come by, then?"

"Planning on it."

"When?"

"Figure on me arriving around eight-thirty."

"Awesome. I'll have plenty of time to feed the horses and the chickens. I should be able to turn the horses out, too. Like I said, come on in the front door. I'll be waiting."

His body heated up. Time to change topics or he'd need another shower. "I forgot to ask. Did you contact anyone about the fox?"

"I did, but I need the pictures from your phone to make a complete report."

"Shoot. I could have sent you those on Saturday when it was slow."

"We can take care of it tomorrow. But let's not get into the fox thing until after we have a chance to—"

"Don't worry." And just like that, he couldn't breathe and his jeans pinched something terrible. His chuckle was a little ragged. "I have my priorities straight."

"Then I'll see you in the morning. I should let you go. You said you were tired."

"Not so much, now."

"All the same, you should go to bed. I will, too."

"Thinking of you going to bed doesn't help."

"I'm trying to decide if I should wear my sexy nightgown in the morning. Do you want me to?"

"Don't see the point." He should end this call before he did serious damage to his privates. "I might rip it."

"Really?"

"The way I'm feeling right now, I just might. I advise you to leave it off."

"You're that excited about seeing me again?"

"Yes, ma'am. And I'm going to say goodnight before my condition gets any worse."

"Do you have blue balls?"

He choked on a laugh. "Where'd you hear that? No, don't tell me. I don't want to know."

"But do you?"

"Not yet. Which is why I'm hanging up, now. Goodnight, Kendall. See you in the morning." He forced himself to disconnect. Talking to her was torture, but not talking to her was also torture, just a different kind.

He stared at his screen. All those texts. But his family didn't know he was standing in front of the firehouse looking at his phone. He could be dealing with firefighter things and unable to answer their texts.

Silencing his phone, he walked back into the station, took off his jacket and crawled into his bunk. But the minute he closed his eyes, the image of Kendall gathering sexual advice from his mother and Marybeth lodged in his brain. Now he'd never get to sleep.

* * *

But he did sleep, courtesy of the day's strenuous physical activity. He woke at dawn and was showered, shaved and sipping coffee in less than twenty minutes. Ranch life had conditioned him to be an early riser and he couldn't break the pattern even when he had no horses to feed.

Kendall would be up by now, too. She did have horses to feed, and chickens. He'd miss that show today, but he intended to catch it tomorrow. Theoretically he could stay at her place until he had to report for duty four days from now.

Would that be a mistake, staying there that long? Probably, although he wanted to and he had no doubt she'd want him to. On the other hand, he couldn't ignore the potential for misunderstandings.

She might interpret such a thing as proof that they were bound for the altar. When she'd still been small, maybe first of second grade, she'd announced to him that they would get married as soon as she was old enough.

He'd like to believe he treated her announcement with kindness, but he'd been a typical clueless boy, so chances were good he'd laughed. Surely she'd abandoned that childhood fantasy by now.

But maybe not. If he asked to stay four days straight, that could send the wrong signal. He was her first lover, but he sure as hell didn't expect to be her last. She deserved to sow some oats before picking a life partner. He'd have a talk with her today and make sure they were on the same page.

He glanced at the clock. Must be something wrong with it. Surely more than ten minutes had passed. He checked his phone. Nope, the clock was right. Slowest ten minutes ever.

He could answer his family's texts. Pulling up two from his mom, he started reading.

Be careful, son. I doubt you're in love with her, but she's head-over-heels. You'll hate yourself if you break her heart. If you'd never in a million years marry her, tell her now.

He sighed. Good advice. He moved to the second one.

PS—Clearly you treated her with tenderness and respect during this important episode. She's grateful for that. So am I.

He texted back, thanking her for solid advice he promised to heed. Then he scanned the ones from everyone else. They all took the same cautionary tone except for Clint, who said *I hope you know you're an idiot. This won't end well.*

Grinning, he texted back. *Thanks for the loving support, bro.* And that was all the time he had as crew members wandered out looking for coffee. He put his phone away.

Ralph arrived early, before the breakfast dishes were cleared, and sent Cheyenne out the door. He didn't argue the point. Arriving at Kendall's earlier than planned was fine with him.

As he pulled out of the parking lot, he checked the gauges. Dammit. If he didn't gas up he could run out before he made it to Kendall's. So much for arriving early.

He paced while the gas gurgled into the tank. She'd had time to recover a bit from the first go-round, but he'd still take it easy today, no matter what she said. Or what he wanted.

Maybe one of the ladies had cautioned her about overdoing. That gabfest on Saturday made his gut clench, but Kendall was smart to gather information from other women. They'd certainly know better than he would about… most things.

He'd never conducted a relationship with so little privacy and never cared to do it again.

Having his entire family on the sidelines offering comments and advice had him second-guessing his every move. But his mother was right. He'd handle Kendall's tender heart with care. Breaking it wasn't an option.

12

Kendall listened so hard for the rumble of Cheyenne's truck that her eardrums vibrated with a steady hum like bees lived in there. At least that was her explanation. As she lay scrubbed, lotioned and naked under her freshly washed sheets, the buzz spread from her ears to her scalp, from her scalp to her lips, from her lips to her breasts.

She turned her head on the pillow and checked the digital clock on the nightstand. 8:26. Four minutes to go. If he arrived exactly on time.

They'd have morning sex. Again. Penny was a big fan of morning sex since that's when she and Sky had started their love affair.

Jess was the opposite. Beau had decorated the bed with fairy lights to make their nighttime sex magical. Angie said anytime was great with the right guy.

Marybeth preferred lazy Sunday afternoons. Desiree's favorite memories involved a blanket in a meadow on a starry summer night. Kendall had made a list. She wanted to try them all.

The clock turned over to 8:27. Was that a truck on the road? *Yes.* Shivering, she filled her buzzing ears with the sweet growl of Cheyenne's truck as it drew closer... closer... and... he was here.

He switched off the engine. Her heart pounded so loud she almost didn't catch the slight creak of the driver's door opening, but the slam as he closed it made her jump. He clattered up the steps and stomped across the porch.

Men are visual creatures. Let him see you. Everyone had agreed on that. Rapid footsteps brought him to her bedroom doorway, where he paused as if to let his eyes adjust.

She flung back the covers. "Here I am!"

His chuckle was a little hoarse. "Yes, ma'am. There you are." He tossed his hat on the dresser and began ripping off his clothes. "What a beautiful sight."

"You, too." He took her breath away. Literally. She was a little fuzzy-headed from lack of oxygen. She sat up so she could breathe better.

"Going somewhere?" He was down to his jeans and had the belt undone.

"I had trouble breathing." She pulled in a bunch of air. Better.

His chest heaved. "That makes two of us. Maybe we should slow the heck down."

"Please don't."

"Yeah, the hell with that." He shoved off his jeans and briefs, revealing the intimate parts.

"Magnificent." Had she said that out loud? Evidently so, because he smiled.

"Glad you approve." He walked to the side of the bed where she'd left condoms in the nightstand drawer. "I need to suit up first thing.

Next time I won't be so quick about doing that, but—"

"Be quick about it." She flopped back on the bed. "I'm desperate."

"I like that in a woman." He tore open a package.

"That's what everyone said. That eagerness makes up for—"

"Tell me later." He rolled on the condom, climbed in and moved over her. "Right now let's concentrate on this." Maneuvering between her thighs, he tucked his big hands under her bottom, lifted her up and sank his cock in as far as it would go.

She gasped. And climaxed. Just like that. As the tremors claimed her, she made a funny wailing sound, grabbed his buns and dug her fingers into his tight muscles.

His expression turned to stone and his breath hissed out through clenched teeth. Squeezing his eyes shut, he maintained his position as sweat popped out on his forehead.

Gradually the ripples slowed and she loosened her hold on his behind. But she didn't let go. She might never let go. Cupping his backside was way too much fun.

As her body relaxed, he let out a groan and opened his eyes. "Wasn't expecting that."

"Are you sure you're not in pain?" A drop of sweat landed on her cheek. "Your face got all scrunched up again."

He gave her a lopsided smile. "I'm not in pain." Leaning down, he licked the drop from her cheek. Then he kissed her gently and lifted his head. "I welcome the challenge."

"I'm a challenge?"

"Yes, ma'am. Not many ladies come that fast. Usually I have time to get my bearings before the fireworks start."

"Like I said before, you should just come, too."

He chuckled. "It's not manly."

"Who cares? I don't."

"Well, I do. I'll be more prepared next time."

"Then so will I. You've learned how to hold back, so you can teach me the same thing."

"God, no. That's the last thing I want. Or you should want. Your responsiveness is a wonderful gift."

"And yours isn't?"

"Yes, but we can have more fun if I control it. You can have several orgasms in a row without reloading, but I only get one. Then time has to pass before I can do it again."

"I know that, but I'm fine with each of us having just one. That's more fair and you don't have to work so hard."

He laughed. "It's not work."

"Sure it is. You're sweating. And by the way, when you laughed that felt nice."

"Oh, did it, now?" He eased back and slid forward again. "Think maybe you're ready for another climax?"

"On one condition."

He grinned and moved back and forth some more. "Setting conditions, are we?"

Oh, boy. He had her going again. "Promise you'll come, too. Otherwise, I'll…" She lost her train of thought as he began a slow, steady rhythm.

"You'll what?"

"I'll hold back, too. It'll be a standoff."

"Are you sure you can back up that threat?" He increased the pace.

"No, but I'll do my damnedest."

His gaze softened. "Okay, I promise." His breath hitched. "I don't want you to hold back. When you came right away, it made me feel like a million bucks."

"And when you come this time, I'll feel like a million bucks."

"I believe you." The light in his eyes intensified. "So let's go for it." Shifting his position, he grasped her hips and pumped faster.

The flexing of his muscles under her palms added an erotic layer that sent arrows of heat straight to her core. She gasped as the spring wound tighter. "Cheyenne…"

"I'm here." He sounded almost gruff.

She looked up. "Your eyes are open."

"Uh-huh." He sucked in a breath. "Ready?"

"Yes." The first spasm hit her. "*Yes.*" Another spasm, and another. "*Now.*"

"Yes, ma'am." He stroked once, twice, and pushed deep with a guttural cry.

Arching upward, she increased the pressure and her world turned upside down, sideways, backward and twirled in a circle. She yelled louder than she did on the Tilt-a-Whirl at the state fair.

Then she started laughing, because she was way happier than she'd ever been on the Tilt-a-Whirl. She was way happier than she'd ever been, period.

Breathing hard, Cheyenne lifted his head and gazed down at her. "Have fun?"

"You know it, buster. Big fun."

He smiled. "Me, too."

"See how perfect it is when we both come together? That's how we should do it all the time."

"I dunno, Sunshine. You'd be giving up a lot of treats."

Pleasure zinged through her at the casual endearment. "Why'd you call me that?"

He looked perplexed. "Just came out. Seems to fit you. Don't you like it?"

"I do like it." She loved it. He'd given her a special name. Her heart was doing jumping jacks. "Do you call anybody else Sunshine? Like Angie?"

"No, ma'am. I can't recall ever using that name for anyone."

"Well, it's mine, now. I've got dibs."

"Fine with me." He dropped a quick kiss on her mouth and eased out of bed. "Need to take care of the condom. Be right back."

"I'll be here."

"Counting on it."

After he was out of sight she gave herself a hug. Things were going great.

And would continue that way if she had anything to say about it. She just had to remember

what Angie had told her privately on Saturday—
*Whatever you do, don't mention the M word. If he
asks if you're hoping for that, tell him it's not even on
the radar.*

   Kendall loved Angie's clever phrase — *not
even on the radar.* So true. Marrying Cheyenne
wasn't some blip on the horizon of her life. It was
securely lodged in her heart waiting for the right
moment to burst free.

13

Cheyenne washed up a bit before coming back into the bedroom. One look at Kendall lying there only half covered by the sheet made his cock twitch. *Down boy. Too soon.*

"I saw that."

"Never you mind."

"I learned on Saturday that every guy has a different recovery time. What's your average?"

He choked on a laugh.

"I only ask because the recovery seems to be starting already and it's been less than ten minutes."

He cleared his throat. "Did you also learn that someone new to sex would be wise to pace herself?"

"Yes, I heard that." She sighed. "And they said you'd be considerate of my situation."

"Which is true."

"But you're almost recovered. It seems a shame to waste—"

"Trust me, it won't be the first time. Let's contact the people about the fox."

"I don't have my phone in here. Why don't we just snuggle for a while and see what happens?"

"You know exactly what will happen."

She smiled. "You want to. I can tell. And if you want to, then I want to."

"Where's your phone? I'll fetch it."

"There's a phone holder on the kitchen counter."

"I'll get it." He walked out and gave his cock a talking to on the way to the kitchen. Helped some.

The kitchen smelled like sugar cookies. He lifted the lid on her cookie jar, a ceramic one shaped like a big red apple, and breathed in. She'd baked a fresh batch. For him.

"Caught you with your hand in the cookie jar."

He turned. She wore his shirt and nothing else. She hadn't bothered with the buttons, either. "Nice outfit."

"I got this idea from a movie. Always wanted to try it." She glanced at his crotch. "Seems you like this look."

"I do." Especially the way she carried it off, her short curls sticking out every which way courtesy of hot sex and her cheeks pink as a morning sunrise. But it was the gleam in her gray eyes that got to him the most. A knowing gleam. And he'd put it there.

The shirt hung over her breasts, but her taut nipples dented the soft material. The aromatic blend of aroused woman and fresh cookies guaranteed he'd be ramrod straight in no time.

Her attention returned to his bad boy. "Why don't we tackle the fox problem later?"

He took a deep breath. Clearly she was fascinated by her newfound power to give him an erection. Which in turn aroused her. She didn't understand, at least not yet, that mutual arousal didn't require immediate action.

But if he said that, it could come off as a rejection. Especially in the heat of the moment. She was so adorably eager to please and be pleased that he'd hate to dampen her enthusiasm. "Seems I have two fox problems."

She lit up. "Good one! I've always wanted to be called a fox."

"Oh, you're a fox, alright." He replaced the lid on the cookie jar and closed the distance between them. "And now we're both hot and bothered. What are we going to do about that?"

She reached down and fondled him. "I have an idea."

"Me, too." Scooping her up, he carried her toward the bedroom.

"Yay! We agree!"

"Not exactly." She was heaven in his arms. And she would be again. Later. He carried her through the bedroom and into the bathroom.

"What are you doing?"

He stepped into the walk-in shower, set her down and pulled her close.

"You want to have sex in here?"

"No, ma'am." Maintaining his grip with one arm, he reached around her. "I'm cooling us down." He turned on the cold water.

She screeched and tried to get loose.

He held on. "Stick with me. This works."

"But I wanted—"

"Believe me, so did I." He put his back to the spray, shielding her a little and letting the icy water freeze his butt, which in turn took care of the rest, despite having her sweet body pressed close. "Seeing you in my shirt really got me going."

She gazed up at him. Her hair was soaked and drops of water clung to her eyelashes. "Now your shirt's wet. And clammy."

"It'll dry."

"I guess you don't need it if we stay in bed."

"Before we go back there, we need to talk."

"About what?" She looked extremely cold.

"Sex."

"While we're being sprayed with ice water?"

"That depends. Do you still have the urge?"

"N-not so much."

"Then I have a big favor. Would you please dry off and get dressed? I'll follow a little later. After your tempting body is covered up."

"C-can't we talk in bed? I'll keep the sheet over me."

"I mean covered up with things that button and zip."

She sighed. "If you insist, I'll d-do it. I'm freezing."

"That was the idea." He let her go. "Call out when you're dressed."

"Okay." She stepped onto the bath mat, pulled a towel off the rack and wrapped up in it. "Brrr."

"See you soon."

"Aren't you going to turn off the water?"

"I'll leave it on a little longer, for good measure."

Her gaze traveled over his water-logged body. "I get what they mean about cold showers. They definitely work." She sounded disappointed.

"Yes, ma'am. It was the only thing I could think of. I hope you'll forgive me." For dunking her and for the state of his manly equipment. But rejecting her would have been worse.

"I forgive you. You must have really been desperate to have sex with me."

"I was."

"Not now. You still look nice, though."

"Thank you."

"Would it eventually get wrinkles like your fingertips do?"

"Don't think so."

"You should turn off the water soon, though, just in case." Casting one last look in the direction of his johnson, she headed for the door. "You wouldn't want that."

Once she started rustling around in the bedroom, he turned off the water, stepped on the mat and searched for another bath towel. Wasn't one. He handled the worst of the drips with the dry washcloth on the rack.

When he was no longer in danger of making puddles on the floor, he checked the cupboards. No spare bath towel there, either. The hand towel hanging by the sink was the best he was going to get. He rubbed himself as thoroughly as he could, including the area that she'd become enamored with.

He hadn't counted on her being so fascinated. Should have, maybe, but he hadn't been with a virgin since he was seventeen. Having his teenage girlfriend focused on his pride and joy had been awesome. They'd both been in love with watching it spring to life.

And because they'd had school, after-school jobs, curfews and parents, they'd never had the opportunity to carry on all day and all night. No doubt that would have landed them in Urgent Care.

"I'm dressed," Kendall called out. "Want me to make coffee? And get out the cookies?"

"Great! How about coffee and cookies on the back porch?"

"For old time's sake?"

He chuckled. "You bet, Sunshine." He was pleased with the nickname. He wasn't normally a nicknaming kind of guy, but that one fit perfectly. Good thing she liked it, too.

When he walked into the bedroom, his jeans, briefs and socks were lying in a neat pile on the bed with his boots nearby on the floor. No sign of his soaked shirt. He'd have to go shirtless for this discussion. The morning was warm, but not that warm.

He had only himself to blame. But if he'd paused to remove the shirt, he would have lost the element of surprise. She must not be too mad about the cold shower if she'd offered to make coffee and get out the cookies.

Anyway, shirtless it was. Until he glanced at the bedroom doorknob. She'd hung her bath towel there. He took it. Damp, but better than nothing. Draping it around his neck, he let it hang down over his chest.

Back in his high school jock days, he used to think this was a cool look. He'd hang onto the ends of the towel and puff out his chest as if he'd just finished a strenuous workout.

That pose didn't work for this scenario, so he just walked out with the towel draped around his neck. Probably looked like he was wearing an oversized muffler crocheted by a sweet female relative with zero needlework skills.

Kendall had her hand in the cookie jar this time, fishing out treats to put on a plate. She glanced up, took one look at the towel and giggled. "Shot yourself in the foot, didn't you, cowboy?"

"This is fine."

"Lucky for you, I threw your shirt in the dryer before I got dressed. It won't be completely dry, but neither is that towel. And you'll look much better in a damp shirt than a damp towel."

"I'll go get it."

"Through there." She tilted her head toward a door off the kitchen. "Might as well give that towel a spin while you're at it." Then she paused, a cookie poised in midair, her expression stricken. "You didn't have a towel, did you?"

"I managed."

"I am *so* sorry. I should have realized—"

"You didn't know I would drag you under a cold shower. That's on me."

She held his gaze. "To be honest, I wasn't sure what to do about amenities like that. Putting out two towels seemed presumptuous, like I expected you to be here long enough to need one."

"Fair enough. On Saturday morning we didn't have time to talk about what comes next."

She swallowed. "You mentioned spending your free nights here, but I wasn't sure exactly what you meant."

"I don't have to be back at the station until Friday morning. Depending on how you'd feel about it, I could—"

"Stay until Friday?" Her voice squeaked a little.

"Yes, but if you think four days is too much—"

"Are you crazy? Of *course* I want you to stay with me until you have to report in. I have spare towels. I have plenty of food, but you'll need—"

"Clothes." The anticipation building in his chest told him he wanted this more than he'd been willing to admit. Assuming they'd be clear on what it did and didn't mean. "I'll need my shaving kit. And basic toiletries. But I wasn't going to bring them over until I consulted you."

"I'm all for it."

He blew out a breath. "Good."

"Is that why you think we need to talk about sex? Because you were considering staying until Friday?"

"Something like that."

"Then say no more. Even I know you can't have sex every hour on the hour over a four-day stretch. That would kill you."

That pricked his ego. "Maybe not, but you'd—"

"Are you nuts? Never mind me getting sore. Your whackadoodle would fall off."

He laughed. "Never heard it called that."

"I just made it up. Makes me smile. Anyway, if I'll have you in residence for that long, I'm willing to space things out. This morning I was feeling as if I had to grab my chances when I could." She paused to give him an arch look. "So to speak."

"I'm not going anywhere, except to fetch what I need from my house."

"That makes me very happy. Does that mean we've covered everything you wanted to talk about on the porch?"

"Almost. There's one more thing."

"What's that? Maybe we can settle it now."

"I'd rather wait until we're sitting on the porch." Discussing their sex life had been tricky. Finding out whether she had marriage on her mind without insulting her would take the skill of a diplomat. And a lot of cookies.

<u>14</u>

Four days. As Kendall carried a tray out to the back porch, she sorted through the possibilities of having Cheyenne in her house for that long. They'd already discussed that they couldn't have endless sex, so what would they do besides that?

Cheyenne came out buttoning his shirt. "Thanks for putting this in the dryer. My body heat should finish the job."

"I'm sure it will." He had some powerful body heat. She could feel it clear over... oh, wait, that was *her* body heat giving her the urge to fan herself.

His shirt was still damp enough to cling. How was she supposed to look at that chest and not want to plaster herself against it?

"That's flattering as hell, Sunshine."

Whoops. She lifted her gaze and met his amused one. "Are you sure? Because most women don't like it when a man focuses on their chest."

"Men don't have that issue. Or at least I don't."

"That's a relief. But I need to stop ogling your body. It only makes me want to have sex with you."

He smiled. "Just because you want to doesn't mean you have to."

"It feels like I have to." She peered at him. "Do you feel that way sometimes?"

"Sure." His eyes went a shade darker. "When you look at me like that. When you tell me you want to have sex, I feel like I have to."

"Do you feel that way now?"

"I'm getting there. Which means it's time to sit down, drink coffee, eat cookies, and talk about something else."

"You are so right." Squaring her shoulders, she walked to the glider, plumped the pillows across the back and took her seat. "I'll pour the coffee. That'll give me something to do with my hands."

"And I'll eat cookies." He settled down next to her, his hip and thigh brushing hers. "Keeps my hands and my mouth busy."

"Is that why you ate so many Friday night?" She poured steaming coffee into both mugs.

"Yes, ma'am."

"So cookies and cold showers help you out. What other tricks do you have up your sleeve?"

"Not many. I've never put myself in this position before."

"What position?" She took a sip of coffee and picked up a cookie.

"Other than taking care of the chickens and the horses, we have no barriers to having as much sex as we want."

"That sounds like the setting of a porn movie."

He blinked. "You've watched porn?"

"Angie and I did one night. It was boring. No plot."

"Theoretically, if we let ourselves have all the sex we wanted, we'd get bored."

Her body stirred. "I'm not so sure."

"I'm not, either. You'd get injured long before boredom set in. We can't go that route. Either I need to reconsider my original plan—"

"Please don't."

"Or we have to come up with some distractions." He finished off his cookie and gazed at her. "Like the handyman jobs I thought I would end up doing. What did you have lined up?"

She flushed. "Oh, those."

"You did have jobs in mind, right? If we hadn't ended up in bed Saturday morning, what had you planned for me to do?"

"The usual chores. Mucking out the stalls. Giving Mischief and Mayhem a thorough grooming."

"I would've had that done by noon. Then what?"

"Then...nothing." She took a restorative gulp of warm coffee.

"Nothing? You were going to send me home?"

She gave him a look. "Hardly. After Friday night, I figured you'd find excuses to stick around."

"Is that so?" His eyebrows lifted.

"Am I wrong?"

"You're not wrong." He held her gaze for one sizzling moment before grabbing another cookie. "Then you're telling me there's no list of handyman tasks sitting somewhere?"

"No, but we could create one together."

"Excellent." He polished off the cookie and pulled out his phone. "What about the chicken pen?"

"Sorry, but I'm not crazy about your motion light idea."

"Then let me think some more." He planted his booted foot and began slowly rocking the glider as he sipped his coffee.

She watched him out of the corner of her eye. She'd always loved this thoughtful side of him. Her girlhood dreams had included peaceful scenes like this, the two of them sitting in easy companionship, content to simply be together.

And here they were. Not hugging, not kissing, not getting naked and having sex. This was nice. Not as nice as sex, but lovely, all the same.

"I've got it." He turned to her with a happy smile. "Surround the pen with an electric fence."

"Ouch! I don't want to electrify that little fox. Or anything, really, especially me or the chickens."

"It'll be about six inches away from the chicken wire, and if you only turn it on at night, you and the chickens won't ever have to worry about it."

"What about the wild critters? I don't want to fry them, either."

"You won't. They'll only get a light shock, enough to make them change their mind about tunneling under and breaking into your coop."

"Hm." She gazed at him. "Have you ever touched one when it was on?"

"Yes. It's not that bad. But it's not pleasant, either. The animals will learn to stay away."

"How long will that take to set up?"

"If we head into town within the next thirty minutes, we can have it done before sundown."

"And then we can have sex?"

"Oh, I'm sure. After holding off all day while we organize this fence—"

"We'll be voracious?" Her body warmed.

He laughed. "Yes, ma'am. That about describes it." He grabbed another cookie that disappeared in no time.

Might as well try his remedy. She took a cookie and demolished it. Not what she craved, but like he said, it gave her mouth something to do. She polished off another one and took a calming breath. "That takes care of today. What about the next three days?"

"We still need to send pictures of the fox to… who did you contact?"

"I called the wildlife biology department at UM. Penny suggested it and gave me a name of a professor. Once we send your pictures, there's nothing more to do unless we see the fox again and get more pictures."

"I see."

"We could stake out the chicken pen again tonight."

"I'm all for wildlife research, but I'm not willing to spend another chilly night on the porch with your night vision binoculars when I could be tucked in your four-poster with you."

So much for staying calm. "But it's another distraction to keep us from having too much sex." She laughed. "That seems nuts when you say it out loud."

"Because it is nuts. Tell you what. Let's concentrate on daytime distractions and let the nights take care of themselves. If we work hard enough during the day, we'll be too tired to have sex all night." He paused. "Theoretically."

She shivered with excitement. "We've never done it at night."

"I'm aware."

"I'm not used to sleeping with someone. I mean actual sleeping, not having—"

"I knew what you meant." He ate the next cookie slowly before he turned to her. "The truth is, I'm not used to it, either. I hardly ever spend the whole night."

Her chest tightened. This was important. "Why not?"

"I'm not sure I can explain why. I just don't feel comfortable staying."

"Are you saying you might leave in the morning?"

"I can't see myself doing that. I wouldn't have suggested this four-day stretch if I'd anticipated taking off at dawn."

"Well, I'm glad, but—"

"Maybe it's the morning sex, which is nothing like dating sex. Or because—" He paused to grin at her. "I like to watch you feed the chickens."

"God knows that's a major attraction."

"Well, it is for me. Bottom line, you're a country girl and your place feels a lot like home."

And now she couldn't breathe at all. Was he hearing himself?

He put down his coffee and turned to her. "And that brings up something else I want to talk about. The main thing, really."

"You have the floor."

He hesitated, as if choosing his words carefully. "I love being here right now. It's a special time for you and I'm the lucky guy who gets to share it."

Here we go. Remember what Angie told you. "Why do I feel like the next part will start with *but*?"

His gaze was steady. "Because you're a smart cookie, Sunshine. The truth is, I'm thrilled to have this time with you, but I'm not your forever guy. I think deep in your heart, you know it, too."

"Maybe." And maybe he was the one with his head up his posterior.

"I just want to make sure that you're not thinking the end game will be a proposal."

"Are we talking about marriage?"

"Yes, ma'am, and I would hate for you to get the wrong idea about—"

"Marriage isn't even on my radar." To her credit, she managed to keep a straight face. His relieved expression almost made her lose it, though.

"I'm so glad to hear you say that. You may decide to settle down eventually, but taking time to explore the possibilities is a great idea. Everyone should do that."

She was dying to debate the point, but that wouldn't be in her best interests. "You've clearly done some exploring." And he hadn't found anyone who made him want to stay for breakfast, thank goodness. Until now.

"I have."

"Has it been fun?"

"Well, yeah. Educational. Like I said, I recommend playing the field for a while."

"How soon should I start?"

He blinked, clearly startled. Then he frowned. "I'm not suggesting you rush into anything."

"Oh, good."

"My thought would be to give yourself some time. Wait until you feel ready to branch out."

"Definitely not until after you go back to work, though."

His frown deepened. "That's a little fast." Then he took a deep breath. "But it's really up to you."

"Okay. I'll see how it goes. Having this talk has helped me a lot."

"I'm happy it has." But he didn't look all that happy, poor guy.

He would be, though, eventually. She would see to it.

15

His truck bed full of supplies to complete the electric fence project, Cheyenne turned off the main road headed for Kendall's place.

"When were you planning to pick up your clothes and stuff?"

"I... sort of forgot about it." His brain had been too busy dealing with the prospect of Kendall dating other guys, possibly by next week. She wouldn't act that quickly, though. Would she?

If so, it was his doing. He'd given her the idea by encouraging her to explore the possibilities. He wanted that for her. He truly did. Just not yet.

"We could go now and then double back to my place."

"Good idea." He bypassed her road and drove the half-mile to the Rowdy Ranch turnoff. "You've never seen my house, have you?"

"Sure haven't. Matter of fact, I've only seen Angie's, which I love. Is yours anything like hers?"

"Something like it. We all chose the log cabin look, just different layouts. She went with the light finish and I went darker. Planted two pines out front when I first moved in. Eight years later, they're taller than the house. I love 'em."

"A pair of evergreens sounds wonderful. Better than just one."

"I like things balanced. I put the steps right in the middle of the porch opposite the door. Then I laid a flagstone path out to my parking area."

"It sounds lovely. A different look from Angie's."

"She chose steps on the side so her chairs can sit in an unbroken row. I wanted a swing on one side and a place to eat on the other, so half-and-half works for me."

"You have a table and chairs on your porch?"

"Sure do. There's a nice view of the Sapphires. Normally I just have two chairs at the table, but it's big enough for a couple more."

"Do you have folks over a lot?"

"Some. Mostly family or guys from the firehouse."

She was quiet for a bit. "Listen, I have no business asking this, but—"

"Let me guess. You want to know if I've taken any women there."

"Well, you told me you don't like staying over with them. Did you solve it by bringing them here?"

"You'd think I would, but I didn't. Considered it. Never followed through."

"Did you like these ladies?"

"Sure, I did. We had fun, good conversations, nice meals. But..." He glanced over at her. "I just figured it out. Thanks to you, really."

"Me?"

"You don't get all discombobulated about how you look, even after we've had sex. That first morning you came to the door in your granny gown and didn't stress about your hair or if you had a sleep crease on your cheek."

"Did I have a sleep crease?"

"No, but you wouldn't have cared, right?"

"Nope. Everybody gets those. But I regretted not wearing my flimsy nightgown."

"That's minor compared to what I'm used to. I've dated nice-looking women, but they don't seem to believe they are."

"That's too bad."

"And limiting. If I muss them up with some kissing and fondling, they start worrying about how they look. The woman I finally stopped dating in February would make me wait for her in bed while she dressed in something slinky and fixed her hair and makeup. Like someone was about to shoot a movie."

"Not very spontaneous."

"Not like you, that's for sure. It's why staying with you is no big deal. I—"

"I beg your pardon? It's a very big—"

"I didn't mean that. It's a huge deal. A privilege. But I can relax. You won't wake up in a panic because your hair's sticking out every which way. Or immediately get to a mirror so you can put on makeup. What a relief."

"That's funny. Angie was convinced I needed to start wearing makeup."

"Why?"

"She thought I'd stand a better chance of … getting dates."

"Maybe she's right. I can't speak for other guys. I guess you'll have a chance to test it." And wasn't that a depressing subject? He swung the truck onto the short lane that led to his place. It was visible from the road.

"Oh, how pretty, Cheyenne! Those twin pines look great and I love the color of the logs. It goes with the dark green of the trees."

"Thank you." Her reaction pleased him. "I string lights on the porch railing at Christmas." And why offer that bit of info in May? By December she'd be well into her adventure, sampling what the local guys had to offer.

"I'll bet it's beautiful, especially with the lights reflecting on the snow."

"I like it. Do you put up Christmas lights outside?"

"I do. And inside. I'm a Christmas decorating nut."

"Doesn't surprise me." And he wanted to be there, damn it. Not feasible. He parked the truck and hurried around to help her out. "This won't take me long."

"Does it matter?"

"Guess not. Since we shopped in record time and ate sandwiches on the way home, we should be okay." He took her hand. "Come on in."

She pulled him back. "Before I see it, let me guess what your furniture is like."

He chuckled. "Go for it." She made even the smallest thing entertaining.

"It's big and sturdy, dark wood—"

"Easy guess."

"And it's upholstered in dark green leather."

"Wish it was. I would have loved that. But that was a special order and cost a small fortune. I went with chocolate brown."

"Then you have dark green pillows, or throws, or lampshades. And a braided rug in green tones under the wooden coffee table."

"You nailed it, except the lampshades are sunshine yellow and the pillows have sunflowers on them to go with the lampshades, all Angie's doing." He glanced at her. "Maybe that's where I got your nickname. From the sunshine yellow lampshades."

She smiled. "Works for me if you did. Let's go in so I can see how you arranged things. I know you have a fireplace. I saw the chimney."

"I never considered *not* having a fireplace."

"My dad wasn't a fan, so we don't have one. He was vague about the details, but something in his childhood made him scared of fire."

"It can be very scary." He led her up the steps and kept hold of her hand as he unlocked the door and opened it. "But also comforting on a cold winter night. I love this one." He drew her inside, where a rock fireplace dominated the far wall.

Her breath caught. "I can see why. That stone is impressive. The gold tones are stunning woven through the gray."

"It's from McGregor Lake. I put money into that instead of special ordering the furniture."

"Good call."

"Thanks." He gave her hand a squeeze. "Wander around all you want. I'll go pack some clothes and a toothbrush."

"Take your time. Can I poke around in the kitchen? I'm fascinated by other people's kitchens."

"Be my guest." He hurried down the hall toward his bedroom. A week ago he'd never have said Kendall would be in his house for any reason. Today she was here so he could pack up enough clothes and a few essentials to carry him through a passion-filled, four-day adventure at her place.

He'd never spent that much continuous time with any woman other than his family members. But Kendall... got to him. She was the most refreshing sexual partner he'd ever had and just plain fun to be with. Surprised the heck out of him, but there it was.

Tucking clothes in a duffle along with his shaving kit, toothbrush and toothpaste, he started to zip it up. He paused to add the condoms he had on hand. She had a fair amount in that bedside table drawer, but running out was not an option.

He zipped up the duffle just as voices drifted from the front of the cabin. Clint was here.

He winced. The fat was truly in the fire, now. Hefting the duffle, he walked back to the living room. "Hey, Clint."

"Hey, bro." Clint's attention went straight to the duffle. "Going somewhere?"

He glanced at Kendall. "You didn't mention—"

"It didn't seem like it was mine to tell."

Interesting. She was an open book with him, so why not with his twin? But he liked that she could play her cards close to the vest if necessary. She'd given him the option of spinning the situation any way he chose.

He met Clint's calculating gaze. "Kendall and I decided it'd be more efficient to settle the terms of the auction if I stay at her ranch until I go back on duty Friday morning."

"I can see how that makes sense." Clint ducked his head as if he was fighting laughter.

"Did you need me for something?"

"Just wondered if you'll make it to Mom's tomorrow night." He lifted his head, eyes sparkling with amusement. "Kendall, too, of course."

"What's going on tomorrow night?"

"She's been wanting to celebrate the good news she got last month on her taxes."

"Oh, yeah, the after-taxes party. I forgot about it with the auction thing and—"

"You weren't the only one who forgot. We've all been crazy busy. Turns out the rest of us can make it and we figured you'd be available since you're off-duty."

"Sounds great." He looked over at Kendall. "You okay with that?"

"Of course. I'd love to party with you all."

"Well, good, then." Clint nodded. "I'm glad I stopped. I saw your truck parked in front of the house. Kendall said you're putting up an electric fence to protect her chickens."

"That's right."

"The fence should do the trick. She also mentioned that you might have seen a swift fox?"

"Maybe. Sure looked like one."

"The wildlife folks at UM should be excited about that. Did you get pictures?"

"I did." Setting down his duffle, he pulled out his phone, located the grainy shots and handed the phone to his brother. "Not conclusive, but it was small and definitely not a pup."

Clint studied the pictures. "You just happened to be out there when it showed up?"

Cheyenne gave Kendall a raised-eyebrow glance. She hadn't filled Clint in? She shrugged and her dimples flashed. Cute as hell.

"Kendall asked me to keep watch Friday night after the auction. She wanted to ID the critter who'd been trying to dig under her fence."

"Ah." Clint's gaze flicked back and forth between the two of them, his eyes crinkled with suppressed laughter. "Looks like the plan worked."

"Guess so." Chances were good Clint wasn't referring to chicken predators. So what if Kendall had laid a trap for him and he'd fallen right into it? He wasn't sorry. Far from it.

"I need to get going." Clint handed back the phone. "Gotta make sure Rance hasn't run afoul of Tyra while I delivered party supplies to Mom. See you two tomorrow night about six." He tipped his hat. "Good luck with that fence." He headed out the door.

His soft chuckle drifted back to them just before the door clicked shut.

Kendall smiled. "He thinks this is hilarious."

"Point of fact, I agree with him. You and Angie had my number."

She glanced up at him. "Do you mind?"

"Do I look like I mind?" He picked up the duffle and tucked an arm around her waist, urging her toward the door. "I'm enjoying myself. So much so that I begrudge the time we'll spend at Mom's tomorrow night."

"But we need to go."

"Yes, we do." He let go of her long enough to open the door and usher her through it. "Not going because I'd rather be canoodling with you would be rude."

"And selfish."

"That, too. We'll go. But I'll be watching the clock."

She laughed. "You're terrible! You can't be watching the clock during a family gathering. You'll be teased within an inch of your life."

"I don't care." He wrapped an arm around her waist on the walk to the truck. "Then again, if you're having a terrific time and want to stay late, that's another story."

"I'll have a terrific time. I always do at Rowdy Ranch. But I don't want to stay late."

"That's what I like to hear." Before he helped her into the truck, he pulled her close and give her a quick kiss. "I'm aware you finagled me into your bed, Sunshine. For the record, I'm very glad you did."

_16_

Before starting on the fence, Cheyenne sent his pictures of the little fox to UM. Then Kendall helped him unload the materials for the fence and they worked side-by-side to get it installed.

They made a good team, which surprised her not at all. The McLintock kids had been trained as team players from the get-go, thanks to being raised by Desiree, Marybeth and Buck.

But some were more gifted at it than others. Cheyenne's easy-going nature guaranteed he'd excel at cooperative projects. He was born to be part of a unit, whether that was a family or his firefighting crew.

As the sun hovered near the horizon, he pulled off his work gloves. "That should do it. We just need to test it and see if it's working."

"Let me put the hens in the coop first. I know they're not supposed to be in any danger from the fence, but I'd feel better if they were locked away before we tested it."

"Fine with me. Need help?"

"Thanks, but it's easy. I lure them in with blueberries. I just need to get some out of the kitchen."

"Blueberries?" His eyes lit up.

"Yep, they love them." She started toward the back porch.

"Ever make blueberry muffins?"

She glanced over her shoulder. "Not that often, since it's just me, but—"

"I'd be glad to help you eat 'em."

His eager expression, lit by the golden glow of sunset, melted her heart. They could be so happy together. She swallowed the response she longed to give him — *marry me and you'll get all the muffins you can handle.*

Angie would have a fit if she allowed impatience to ruin the program when everything was going smooth as silk. "How about a batch of muffins for breakfast?"

"Terrific. I'd love that. I'll help. I'm good in the kitchen."

"I'm sure you're good in every room in the house."

He laughed. "I'm sure you are, too. Better get a move on before I follow you in there."

Heady stuff. "Gotcha." High on her sexual power, she dashed into the kitchen, fetched a bowl of berries and started back to the pen.

Too bad she hadn't worked up the courage to seduce him years ago. Better late than never, though. He—where'd he go? As tall as he was, he should be easy to spot, and yet.... She walked past the chicken coop and scanned the area. No sign of him.

"I'm down here, talking to the ladies."

She looked over. "So you are." The coop had blocked her view of Cheyenne inside the pen, sitting on his heels, hands resting on his knees. Loretta kept her distance, her glossy black feathers ruffled, but Dolly and Reba strutted back and forth in front of him making throaty little noises.

"I figured I owed them an apology. They missed story hour."

"You remembered that?"

"Not the sort of thing a guy can forget. M.R. Morrison's westerns are action-packed. I hope you didn't leave these ladies hanging in the middle of a shoot-out." He glanced up, the teasing light in his blue eyes sexy as hell.

"I didn't." Assuming they could have kids, he was going to make an amazing father. "Seemed like a cheap trick to play on those chickens since I knew you'd show up today and story hour might not happen." She let herself into the pen and immediately two hens hurried in her direction. Loretta lagged behind, but not as far behind as the day before.

"I tried to explain it was for a good cause. I didn't describe our project in detail, though. Didn't want to freak them out."

"Good thinking."

"They're more social than I expected, at least Dolly and Reba." He stood. "Loretta would prefer I vamoose."

"She's only just beginning to warm up to me." Crouching down, she tossed blueberries to her ladies. "Isn't that right, Loretta?" She tossed one to the black hen, then another one onto the ramp. Loretta ran for it and then hurried inside. Dolly and Reba would need more coaxing.

"Now, see, they're doing the same thing to you they did with me, cocking their heads and giving you that unblinking, hairy eyeball stare, like they think you're full of it."

"They don't blink much. Not like we do."

"And it's always the right eye. Why's that?"

"Because that's the near-sighted one." She got to her feet and walked over to the coop. "That's not to say they don't think I'm full of it, but—"

"I doubt they feel that way about you, but that's exactly what they think of me. They're just waiting for me to screw something up."

"Or they're recording your face."

"That I would believe, too. And sending it to some poultry database in preparation for the day the chickens take over. I'd be at the bottom of the pecking order."

"Ha-ha."

"Seriously, why do they give me that look as if I'm under surveillance?"

"You are, in a way. They're prey and you have the eyes of a predator. They can see you better with that eye. The left eye is far-sighted for airborne threats like hawks."

"No kidding? That's very cool."

"Chickens are extremely cool."

"So if they saw a hawk overhead, they'd make tracks for the coop?"

"That's the idea." Humming *Taps,* she laid berries all the way up the ramp and reached through the door to scatter some inside. "Since all three have survived so far, I'll assume they're doing that. We have plenty of hawks in the neighborhood."

"Ever considered putting wire over the top of the fence to keep them out?"

"I have, but I'd either have to raise the height of the fence quite a bit or be willing to duck-walk when I'm inside. I'd rather depend on their left-eye survival skills."

"Simpler that way." He stood by as she tossed more blueberries inside. "Dolly doesn't wanna go in."

"She's the most resistant. If she had complete freedom, she might be fine outside the coop. She could probably outsmart a predator. But her options are limited in this pen. Okay, Dolly, in you go. That's a good girl." She gave the golden-feathered hen a nudge, closed the door and locked it. "Done."

"I like that you hummed *Taps* while you coaxed them in. That has flair."

"It's also part of the conditioning. Treats and a familiar sound or command will become their automatic cue to file into the coop."

"The more I see what work you've put into those chickens, the more I appreciate the omelets you made Saturday morning."

She stood. "It's worth it to me. And it's kind of you to help me find ways to protect them."

"Speaking of that, it's time to test the fence."

"How?"

"I'll turn it on, grab the wire and see what happens."

"You will not!"

He grinned. "No, I will not." He went over and turned on the switch he'd installed earlier. "Should be live."

"You're not grabbing it."

"No, ma'am." He plucked a long blade of grass from a cluster near the pen. "I just touch the grass to it, keeping my hand back six or seven inches, then move my hand up gradually until I feel something." He gradually shortened the distance until he paused. "There. We have juice."

"Did you get shocked?"

Tossing the grass away, he nudged back his hat and puffed out his chest. "Some, but I can take it."

Laughing, she walked over and wound her arms around his neck. "You're so manly and brave."

"Thank you for noticing." He pulled her close and leaned down to kiss her. "This is only a stop-gap measure. We still have horses to round up and feed before we can go inside and get busy. I just need one kiss to tide me over."

Her heart played a happy tune. "You can have two."

"If I take two, I might end up carrying you inside and the whole program will fall apart. One kiss. That's enough for now." His lips found hers.

She sighed with pleasure and relaxed into the arms of her true love. Someday, maybe soon, she'd be able to tell him that. But first he had to figure out that she was his true love.

For now, she'd savor the restrained passion behind this kiss that he was determined wouldn't go anywhere. But it was going somewhere, racing through her system like wildfire, heating her blood and dampening her panties.

When he thrust his tongue into her mouth, she wiggled against him and discovered their kiss was going somewhere in his body, too, mostly the area behind his fly.

He abruptly ended the kiss and backed away with an exasperated sigh. "Damn, woman. I don't know how you do it, but you get me riled up faster than any lady I've known."

She smiled. "You get me riled up faster than any man I've ever known."

"Well, that makes sense. You've only known one man, whereas I've..." He paused and cleared his throat.

"Go on." She gazed at him in fascination. "Now I'm curious. How many?"

"Never mind. That's not important."

"Evidently it is if you're trying to figure out why I have this effect on you."

"I'm just puzzled, is all. I honestly thought I could steal a kiss before we went to catch the horses. I've kept my hands to myself all afternoon because we needed to finish the project, and I've missed holding you, so I..." His voice trailed off as he sent her a searing glance. "And now I want you so bad I can taste it."

She gulped. "And?"

"Unless you object, I'll take care of the horses by myself. I'll be in to take a shower after I'm done."

"A cold shower?"

He gave her a tight smile. "I could use one right now."

"Sorry, not sorry."

"I'm not sorry, either. Just... confused."

"Go ask Mischief and Mayhem. They might have some answers for you. Meanwhile I'll go take a nice warm shower and put on something comfortable."

"Not the slinky nightgown, please. Usually the material of those is no fun to touch."

"Do you prefer flannel?"

"Yes, yes, I do. And now I'm leaving while I can still walk." He turned, wincing and muttering under his breath as he lengthened his stride.

Poor guy. The answer was obvious. Either he couldn't see it or he stubbornly refused to. She'd have to wait him out. Not such a bad prospect.

_17_

Cheyenne would have talked to Mischief about the issue, man to stallion, but man to gelding didn't work. Mayhem had experience in such matters, but from the female side of things. Cheyenne was looking for guidance from another male.

Once he had both horses in their stalls, he called Clint and tucked the phone between his ear and shoulder as he fetched a hay flake for Mayhem. Ladies first.

"I shouldn't answer this." Background noise from the Buffalo in full swing meant this conversation with Clint would have to be short and to the point.

"I'm in trouble, bro."

"I could tell that when I saw you two this afternoon. You're hooked on her."

"I know, but it's more than that. I want her more than I want to breathe."

"Could see that, too. Tomorrow night at Mom's should be fun. Hold on a sec." The sound of happy people was muffled as Clint spoke to someone, probably a member of the staff.

Cheyenne fetched a hay flake for Mischief. As he dropped it into the hay net, muffled sounds from his phone stopped and Clint came on.

"Okay, I'm back. So you're in trouble because you're ass-over-teakettle for little Kendall Abbott."

"Right! For *Kendall Abbott*. I've been avoiding her for years. Now I can't get enough. What's up with that?"

"I have a theory."

"Let's hear it. I'm a desperate man."

"Am I right that you're her first?"

"Yes, sir. But if you think she's shy and retiring, she's not the least bit—"

"I wasn't thinking that. Not with the way she bid on you — I mean, me — at the auction."

"Are you sure your sexy dance didn't flip some switch in her brain? Because she's—"

"It's not me, bro. It's you she's after, has been for years. You're her dream man. We all knew that."

"Okay, okay. That explains why she's infatuated with me. It doesn't explain why I'm bat-shit crazy about *her*."

"It's the lure of the exotic, buddy. You haven't been with a first-timer since... what, high school?"

"Yep. And we were both clueless."

"But you're not anymore. You're the expert and she's the novice. What guy wouldn't get turned on by that setup?"

"I hadn't looked at it that way. Makes sense, though. She's damned good for my ego."

"Just stay alert if she starts talking marriage. You don't want your ego tricking you into something that's not right for you."

"We've already been over that."

"You have?"

"I asked her point-blank if she thought this would end up with me proposing because I had no such intentions. She said that wasn't even on her radar."

"Surprising. I would have sworn that was her goal. But maybe now that she knows sex is fun, she may have a hankering to find out what brand of entertainment others can offer."

Cheyenne's jaw clenched. "Yep. And she should."

"You don't sound thrilled about the prospect."

"I just don't want her to get hurt. You know as well as I do that guys can be—"

"And she needs to learn that, the same way we've had to learn that not every woman means what she says. Or says what she means. Listen, I need to go, so can we—"

"Sure, bro. I'll just blame my over-active ego. That helps. Thanks."

"You're welcome. See you two tomorrow night. I'm looking forward to it."

"Promise me you won't point and laugh."

"Not to your face." Clint disconnected.

Tucking his phone back in his pocket, Cheyenne checked to make sure Mischief and Mayhem were happily munching away. Paying a visit to each of their stalls, he gave them a pat and wished them a good night.

He would have an excellent night, no question. But thanks to Clint, he had a handle on his situation. Sort of embarrassing really, that Kendall's starry-eyed appreciation for his sexual prowess could turn him inside out.

He'd told her being her first was a privilege, and it was, but evidently it fired up his rocket more than a little. Clint was right about that. If anyone had asked him if he'd react that way, he'd have denied it.

Now that Clint had identified the reason for his fixation, he just had to wait for the effect to wear off. But what if she decided to move on before that happened? Ah, hell, not likely. He was, after all, pretty good at this.

Dusk had fallen and lights were on in the house. He walked faster. Kendall was inside, waiting.

Was she wearing her granny gown? God, he hoped so. Her naked body covered in soft flannel decorated with sprigs of flowers created an irresistible combo of wholesome and erotic.

The urge to charge in there and ravish her was strong. She might even like that. Hell, of course she would. He could do no wrong, at least for now. Yep, his ego was swelling right along with his cock.

But he would take a shower first. Just because she wouldn't care if he was fragrant and sweaty, she deserved his best effort.

Taking the steps two at a time, he walked in the kitchen door. And almost lost it.

She stood by the stove in her granny gown, feet bare, cheeks flushed as she stirred some delicious smelling pot of food. Images of kitchen-counter sex heated his blood to the boiling point.

She glanced his way, her expression inviting him closer. "Welcome back."

He couldn't respond. He was too busy keeping himself nailed to the spot when every fiber of his body yearned to sweep her into his arms and love her until they were both exhausted.

Her lips curved in a smile that created the dimples that drove him wild. "You look kind of manic."

"Because..." He cleared the lust from his throat. "Because I am."

"I left you some hot water. But if you want to skip your shower, I can turn off the burner and let this simmer."

"I'm taking a shower." Summoning what little control he had left, he stalked past her, his arms at his sides. "But you'd better turn off the stove."

"Want me to wait for you in bed?"

"Yes, ma'am. Please." He left quickly and ignored the pain behind his fly. Speeding through the bedroom, he glanced at the bed.

She'd turned back the covers. Not a big thing, but he cherished it. He breathed in the sweet scent of her soap and shampoo that filled the bathroom. She'd remembered to add another bath towel and a second washcloth.

He stripped down, groaning as he freed his eager and very stiff friend. The warm shower was heaven and hell. The water sluicing over him felt like gently teasing fingers, coaxing him to let go. Not yet.

Gritting his teeth, he soaped up, rinsed and shut off the water in record time.

"I hope I left you enough hot." Her voice drifted in from the bedroom.

"I'm so hot it might've been cold water for all I know." He took the towel from the rack and began scrubbing it over his sensitized body. "Did you leave on your granny gown?"

"I did."

He hung up the towel and walked out of the bathroom. She was propped up on the pillows set against the headboard, looking like the demure maiden she certainly was not. He took a moment and tried to quit shaking.

She swept her gaze over him. "There's one thing from the porn movie we haven't tried yet."

"Only one?"

"Only one that interests me, and they do it a lot so I got the gist. The others looked too complicated. And usually involved multiple folks." She tossed back the covers on what now seemed to be his side, next to the condom drawer. "Come lie on your back."

"You want to be on top?"

"That's not it. I guess there are two things we haven't tried. That's the other one."

He approached the bed, still a little shaky from wanting her, not particularly confident regarding his self-control. He reached for the drawer handle. "Maybe I should get—"

"You don't need one for what I have in mind." She patted the mattress. "Come on down."

He held her gaze, understanding penetrating his testosterone-drenched brain. "Are you..." Heat shot through him.

"Yes. You're about to enjoy my first attempt at a blow job."

He gulped and shook his head. "Not a good time. I won't last two seconds."

"That's why I want to try it, now. Guaranteed success."

"You'll always have that. We can try it later."

"Cheyenne..." She gave him a look. "Are you afraid you'll embarrass yourself?"

"I'm not—" But she'd hit the nail on the head. If he came immediately, which was likely, his precious ego would suffer. Enough of that. He slid onto the mattress and stretched out.

She scooted around, her flannel gown brushing against his side as she got into position. Tantalizing.

She ended up cross-legged opposite the object of her attention. But instead of reaching for it, she picked up his clenched fist. "Relax." She massaged his wrist and hand until he slowly uncurled his fingers. "That's better." She kissed his palm. Then she ran her tongue around it.

His breath hitched.

"Did that get to you?"

"Everything you do gets to me."

"That makes me happy. Now I'm going to make you happy. At least I hope so. Here goes." She gripped his cock firmly, leaned over, took almost the full length into her mouth and began to suck.

He almost blacked out. Then he came, his breathing sounding like he'd slipped a gear. She stayed put, swallowing everything he gave her.

The room spun. He lost track of time. Gradually his heartbeat sounded less like a guy running from an enraged bull and more like a guy who was recovering from the swiftest, most intense oral sex experience of his life.

Her warm mouth gave way to cool air. "Did you like it?"

He dragged in a breath. "Spectacular."

"You were right that it would be fast. Are you embarrassed?"

"I'm too blissed-out to be embarrassed."

"Oh, good. Because I liked making you come right away. It made me feel powerful and sexy."

Sound familiar, dude? "I'm glad. That's a great feeling. The only downside is you totally melted me. I need to lie here a while until I can pull myself back together."

"Thanks to you, I know just what that's like. Take your time." Sliding down beside him, pressing her granny-gown covered body against his, she laid her arm across his chest. "We'll just talk."

18

Kendall had fantasized moments like this, cuddling in bed with Cheyenne while they discussed the news of the day, their plans for the future, and the goings-on of his large family.

"What would you like to talk about?" His voice was relaxed and lazy, his breathing even.

"The bachelor auction."

He sighed. "Not my finest hour."

"Did you ever intend to go on stage Friday night or was Clint your work-around from the beginning?"

"I tried to convince myself I could do it. The rest of the single guys loved the idea and it was for a good cause."

"What stopped you?"

"I have zero talent for that Chippendale's stuff. I was willing to suffer the humiliation of being bad at it, but what if my moves were so lame nobody bid on me? Then we might not raise enough money."

"I would have bid on you."

He chuckled. "And you'd have paid a lot less than you had to after Clint sashayed around up there."

"I didn't care what I paid. Like you said, it was for a good cause." With her arm resting lightly over his chest, she could feel the steady beat of his heart. Wonderful.

"How soon did you figure out it wasn't me?"

"Right away."

"Because Angie and Mom guessed?"

"We all figured it out about the same time."

"It was his hair. He was gonna get a trim so it was closer to my length. He didn't have time."

"It wasn't that."

"What, then?"

"He doesn't look like you."

"The heck he doesn't. We've been fooling people for years. We did it again Friday night. Sure, my family caught on right away, and the guys from the station did, too, but I doubt anybody else knew."

"I can always tell when it's you or Clint."

"How?"

"You have that tiny scar on your chin. He doesn't."

"You could see that from where you were sitting?"

"Well, no, but his lower lip isn't quite as full as yours. And he has a tiny mole on his forehead, up near the hairline. Usually it's covered by his hat."

"C'mon. You couldn't see that kind of detail Friday night."

"I could see his mouth, and knew it wasn't your mouth. That was enough for me. Besides, I had trouble believing you'd get up there in the first place, so trading with Clint made perfect sense."

"Maybe you couldn't imagine me doing it, but until Thursday night, I was determined to follow through."

"But in the end, you found a way to get out of it and still satisfy the obligation."

"Only because Clint agreed. If he'd said no, I would have been on that stage."

"And hated every second."

"Yes, ma'am."

"Because it's not in your nature. You're a very private person."

He was quiet for a moment. "I suppose I am."

"I'm guessing Clint was the one who mostly suggested trading places when you were younger."

"Matter of fact, he was."

"Did you ever refuse?"

"A few times, but he had a way of goading me into the prank. He got such a charge out of fooling people that I hated to deny him the fun of it."

"So it was unusual for you to instigate a trade."

"Yeah, and that might be one of the reasons he went along with the idea. That and he nearly fell over laughing when I tried out the sexy walk he tried to teach me." He chuckled again. "So did I, after I saw the—" He broke off and cleared his throat.

"The *video*?" She sat up. "Did someone take a video of it?"

"Um, Rance did, but—"

"I suppose you made him erase it. I'm not surprised, knowing you, but I would have *loved* to see it."

He hesitated. "I left my phone on the bathroom counter. At least I think I did. It might still be in the pocket of my jeans. I was a little distracted. Sorry, but my clothes are on the floor. I didn't know what to—"

"The video's on *your* phone?"

"I'm the only one who has it. I made Rance send it to me and delete his version. He and Clint begged me not to destroy it, so I haven't. They promised to let me be the one to decide if it ever saw the light of day."

"Would you mind if I watched it?"

He smiled. "Guess not. After what just happened, there's no point in trying to preserve my dignity."

"Great." She scrambled off the bed. "I won't tell *anybody* about this."

"The video? Or my two-second orgasm?"

"Both." She gazed at him as tenderness engulfed her in a wave. "Your secrets are safe with me."

His expression softened. "I believe you, Sunshine."

The nickname combined with his obvious trust sent a shiver of delight up her spine. Shared secrets brought couples closer together.

His phone lay on the bathroom counter as he'd predicted. His clothes were in a pile on the floor. "I'm dumping your clothes in the hamper."

"You don't have to wash them."

"We'll talk about it later." She carried the phone back to the bed and he sat up as she approached. "You'll have to unlock it for me."

He took the phone. "I'll watch it with you. Maybe it's not as bad as I remembered."

Climbing back in bed, she settled down next to him. "Roll 'em."

He tapped the screen.

She leaned closer. "That's Clint on stage."

"You really can tell?"

"Yep. Your back's to the camera. That's how you stand, with your right hip cocked."

Clint's voice was faint but audible. *Swivel your hips as you come toward center stage, like so. Then pause and do a hip rotation in the middle.*

Ooooo, baby, you're so hot!

Kendall giggled. "You didn't know Rance was shooting this?"

"Wouldn't have been laughing if I'd known. I'd have had him for lunch."

Clint's faint voice again. *You gotta have fun with it. Laugh, smile, loosen up. You try it.*

Cheyenne moved into place. *Here goes nothing.*

As he made his herky-jerky way across the stage, Kendall pressed her lips together to hold back the giggles. Couldn't do it. When Rance came out with his falsetto *Ooooo, baby, you look soooo constipated!* she totally lost it.

Cheyenne was in the same fix. He laughed until he gave himself the hiccups. "I'm *terrible*." Gulping for air, he laid his phone on the nightstand and wiped his eyes with a corner of the sheet. "Even worse than I remembered." His chest jerked with another hiccup.

"Not terrible." She grinned at him. "Adorable."

He rolled his eyes. "That's what you say to a toddler who ate his macaroni and cheese all by himself. With his fingers." Another hiccup.

She straddled him, sitting on his firm abs. "Let's get rid of your hiccups."

"I just need some water."

"You just need this." Cradling his face, she slipped the middle finger of each hand into his ears, leaned forward and kissed him.

"Mm." He pushed the hem of her granny gown up her thighs and cupped her bottom, kneading gently. A hiccup shook him again.

She thrust her tongue into his mouth and tucked her fingers a little deeper into his ears.

With a soft moan, he tightened his grip on her backside and kissed her back, sucking on her tongue.

When she was totally out of air, she gradually pulled away from the kiss, slid her fingers free and took a deep breath. "Hiccups gone?"

"Yes, ma'am." His breath was warm against her mouth. "Great remedy."

"Thanks."

"But I seem to have a new problem."

"Can I help?"

"I do believe you can. Just lean to your right, open the drawer and bring me one of those little raincoats."

"Storm brewing?" She opened the drawer and plucked out a condom.

"Sure is." His heavy-lidded gaze didn't hide the fire smoldering there. He loosened his grip on her backside. "If you'll give that to me and move your sweet tush, I'll prepare for the onslaught."

She ripped open the packet. "I love the sound of tearing open a condom wrapper."

"I'm fond of it, myself." He took a deep breath. "I just need a little space, Sunshine, so I can—"

"I'll do it. Just stay where you are, okay?"

He eyed her. "You'll put it on, right? I don't need another of your spectacular—"

"I'll put it on, I promise." She eased one leg over some impressive evidence that he'd pulled himself back together. She knelt beside him, took the condom out of the package and tossed the wrapper over her shoulder.

"Interesting move." His breathing had picked up considerably.

"You gotta put it somewhere, and I decided throwing it over my shoulder had flair."

"When did you decide this?"

"Last summer, when I was practicing on a zucchini."

His chuckle was slightly raspy, like he might be under a strain. "That's funny."

"You sound a little tense."

"Just impatient."

"Right." Heart racing, she rolled on the condom. "I have to say, you're way more interesting to dress up than a zucchini. Warmer, too."

"Thank you. Can I assume we're going for the other porn movie action you wanted to try?"

"Yes, we are. And it will be more visual for you if I take this off." Grabbing handfuls of the flannel gown, she pulled it over her head.

He sucked in a breath. "Definitely more visual."

She surveyed her handiwork. "I have a general idea how this position works, but you're welcome to give me pointers."

"Step one, climb aboard."

"I kinda knew that." She straddled him again, this time in a more strategic spot, her body humming with anticipation, the ache building deep within her core.

He grasped her hips. "Let me be of assistance."

"Would that turn you on more?"

"I don't think that's possible." His gaze held hers. "I just love touching you."

"Same here." She flattened her palms against the lightly furred expanse of his chest as he coaxed her to lower herself over his waiting cock. "I like this."

"Me, too." Slowly, tenderly, he drew her down.

Heart galloping, she lost herself in blue eyes as they darkened to navy. Her words came out breathy and quivering. "Now what?"

He smiled. "That's the whole point of this position. You're in charge. Whatever feels good to you."

"Oh, my." She took stock. "Staying here feels pretty darn good."

"Uh-huh." His voice lowered to a seductive murmur. "Betcha moving will feel better."

Pressing on his chest, she slowly lifted her hips and slid back down. "Ohhh."

"Told you."

"The..." She gulped for air as her core tightened. "The angle's..."

"More intense?"

She nodded and tried it again, faster this time.

"Nice." His eyes glittered.

Taking a deep breath, she began to move, finding the rhythm, gasping as the tension built with every downward stroke. She closed her eyes, concentrating. There. Right *there.*

His breath hitched and she opened her eyes. The muscles flexed in his jaw. He was holding back.

"Come with me."

He shook his head.

She dragged in a breath. "You said I'm in charge." She moved faster, racing toward her climax. "So you have to—" She cried out as waves of pleasure surged through her. "*Cheyenne.*"

With a deep groan, he thrust upward, holding her gaze as his climax blended with hers. Glorious. After long, delicious moments, the rolling, pulsing wonder of their mutual release slowed.

He sank back to the mattress and a slow grin spread over his beautiful mouth.

"What's so funny?"

"I just realized something about you, Sunshine."

"What's that?"

His grin widened. "You're bossy in bed."

"And?"

"I like it."

19

After rousing himself from the afterglow of satisfying sex, Cheyenne was more than ready for the chicken soup Kendall had left simmering on the stove. She'd made it from Marybeth's recipe a couple days ago.

That meant the flavors had been allowed to mature, as Marybeth liked to say. He ate two bowls along with several slices of homemade bread slathered in butter. When Kendall fetched the cookie jar, he devoured a fair share of its contents, too.

He had visions of making love to her at least once more before they called it a night. Then he looked across the table and caught her smothering a yawn. "Sleepy?"

"I don't want to be sleepy." She sounded annoyed at herself.

A tender emotion that had nothing to do with lust warmed his chest. "It's been a long day. You made dinner. Why don't you go on in and I'll clean up?"

She hesitated.

"Seriously, I'd like to do this. I'll be there soon."

"I'll be waiting."

He smiled. "Nice to know."

She blew him a kiss, turned and headed for the bedroom.

Such a sweet gesture. He couldn't remember any woman he'd been involved with blowing him a kiss. Nothing particularly sexy or suggestive about it. Just... a loving thing to do. A Sunshine thing to do.

He tucked the soup kettle in the fridge. She'd likely made it for him. Probably the bread, too. She had so much to offer those she cared about. He'd been guilty of not paying attention.

No wonder Angie enjoyed spending time here. He did, too. And not just when they were naked. The day had sped by and he'd never once wished he could be somewhere else.

Washing up the dishes didn't take long. Soon he had the kitchen looking tidy, the way Kendall kept it. Her appliances and countertops were much older than his, but he liked the lived-in vibe. Way more cooking went on here than at his place.

A crock of wooden utensils on the counter held more than a dozen items, half of which he'd never use. He'd bet she used them all. Her kitchen smelled better than his, too. Of sugar cookies, yeah, but also baked bread, chicken soup, coffee, and fragrant spices his nose couldn't identify.

Hanging up the dishtowel, he turned off the light and walked toward the soft glow coming from the bedroom. His body tightened in anticipation. How would she greet him this time? Sure was quiet in there.

He walked through the door, a big ol' smile on his face as he reached for the buttons of his shirt. "I'm—" Cutting himself off, he tiptoed over to her side of the bed.

She was asleep. Not playing possum, either, judging by the soft little snore and her slightly open mouth. He'd worn her out.

He shifted his weight and his boot came up against something on the floor. Bending over, he picked up a book that had landed face down on the rag rug when it slipped from her fingers.

He glanced at the title. *Drive Him Wild in Bed*. Yikes. He was already a slave to — what had she called it? — his whackadoodle. She was dynamite as she was. If she started adding embellishments, he was liable to end up in traction.

Laying the book gently on the nightstand, he switched off the lamp and backed away. He undressed in the faint moonlight coming in through the gauzy curtains. Gradually his eyes adjusted and he could see okay.

He was an expert at quietly taking off his clothes in semi-darkness after sharing a room with Clint well into their dating years. Clint hated being jolted out of a sound sleep by a dropped boot or a belt buckle hitting the floor, especially on the rare occasions when Cheyenne had a steady girlfriend and Clint did not.

Luckily the solid oak bedframe didn't creak when he slipped under the covers. He lay quietly listening to her even breathing, sometimes interrupted by a little snuffle.

He'd been in bed with women, but he'd never literally slept with one. The unusual nature of this might keep him awake. If so, he'd stay still and make sure he didn't toss and turn. Kendall needed her rest.

She lay on her right side, facing away from him. Easing carefully to his right side, he gazed at her. Moonlight caught in her curls and reflected on the curve of her ear.

He longed to touch her, but she wasn't used to sharing a bed with someone, either, unless he counted the times Angie had spent the night over here. He might startle her.

She let out a sigh and flopped to her back.

He held his breath. Was she waking up? He waited several seconds. Nope, not waking up. Part of him was glad, but the part below his waist was not.

Maybe it was better that she'd zonked out. While sex with her was satisfying, it only made him want more. Taking breaks should help calm him the heck down.

Now that the fence was done, tomorrow he'd look for other projects around the property. Owning a ranch meant continuous maintenance issues. He'd have no trouble staying busy.

The longer he listened to Kendall's even breathing, the more peaceful he became. Moving his hand over the smooth sheet, he made light contact, his forefinger touching her thumb. Then he closed his eyes and drifted off.

When he opened them again, the pale light of dawn peeked through the curtains. And he had his arms around Kendall. She'd turned to her right side again during the night. Sometime after that he must have wrapped his left arm around her waist and slid his right under the curve of her neck.

That arm might be asleep. He couldn't feel his fingers. Did he care? No, he did not. The pleasure of her soft body nestled against his outranked temporarily numb digits.

"I can hear you thinking, Cheyenne."

"You're awake?"

"Ever since you woke up. I've been waiting for you to bolt."

He drew her closer. "Not going to. I'm sure I'm right about why I used to do that. I didn't want to deal with a woman freaking out about her morning face."

"Wanna see mine?"

"Very much." He let go so she could turn over.

She rolled over to face him and scooted in his direction. "Do I have a pillow crease on my cheek?"

"No." He caressed her warm, sleep-flushed skin. "Maybe because you were propped on my arm." He flexed the tingling fingers of his right hand.

"I laid on your arm all *night*?"

"I have no idea. That's how we were when I woke up."

"Is your hand numb?"

"It was. Not so much anymore."

"But little needles are poking it, aren't they?"

"I don't care."

She frowned at him. "We need some ground rules. I don't want you waking up paralyzed."

He chuckled. "Bossy in bed. I called it last night."

"For your own good, buster."

Tugging her closer, he began kissing her face, although not her mouth. That could lead to full-blown sex and much as he wanted that, he held himself in check. "Rules for you and me in this bed? Do I get a vote?"

"Of course you do."

"Then I vote no rules." He drew back to gaze into her beautiful gray eyes. "We don't need 'em."

Her smile was gentle. "Clearly we do if you'd sacrifice the circulation in your arm because you don't want to wake me up."

"Go easy on me, Sunshine. I'm not used to waking up with someone."

"Neither am I." Her voice was like a spring breeze. "But I like it."

"Full disclosure, I want you again."

"I can tell." Her eyes grew luminous. "But you're not going to do anything about it, are you?"

That settled it. "I'm not, but how do you know?"

"Because we're country folks and we make a commitment to our animals. Or mine, in this case. We're not comfortable lolling around in bed while they're out there waiting, dependent on us for food and fresh water."

He chuckled. "You sound like my mom."

"And mine. She taught me that early on."

"Same here. That might be another reason I didn't stay over on any date. I was raised to get my ass out of bed and down to the barn. Even if I'm in town and there's no barn in sight, I can't sleep past dawn."

"I sure didn't mean to abandon you last night."

"No worries."

"I thought reading that book would keep me awake, especially knowing you'd be in any minute. But when I'm super tired, nothing works." She smiled. "Not even the prospect of sex with you, evidently."

Excellent. His ego could use reminders that he wasn't irresistible, after all. "I wanted to ask about that book..."

"Never mind the book. If we start talking about it, I'll want to grab you. Let's just ignore what's going on under the covers, get dressed and feed the critters."

"I can if you can."

"I can if you stay in bed while I get dressed. I'm weak, Cheyenne. One look and I might make those chickens wait."

Then again, maybe he was just that tempting. "I don't want that on my conscience. Go on." He gave her a little nudge. "Get out of here."

She reached down and gave his cock a squeeze.

He gasped. "Sunshine, for God's sa—"

"Bye for now." She scooted out of bed, pulled some clothes from her dresser and walked toward the bathroom with a taunting sway of her hips.

He groaned in frustration. "You don't play fair."

"I absolutely do." Her voice drifted out of the bathroom. "That was an invitation and I plan to make good on it later today."

"Glad to hear it." He'd look for lighter chores this time, ones that wouldn't leave her too sleepy for after-dinner games. They could... oh, wait. They'd agreed to go to his mom's house tonight. "Don't forget the party."

"I've factored that in."

He smiled. "Okay." Last night he'd mapped out a strategy for today, but clearly she had, too. Should be interesting to see how it played out. "By the way, I want to stick around and watch you feed the chickens. Any problem with leaving Mischief and Mayhem's breakfast until after you're done?"

"That's how I do it when I'm here alone, so no problem at all. I'll go down to the barn with you."

"Perfect. I—" He lost his train of thought as she reappeared.

She was covered up, darn it, in jeans and a long-sleeved Yellowstone T-shirt with a buffalo on the front. "Your turn, cowboy."

When had she gone from cute to stunningly beautiful? "You look terrific."

"Thanks. I'll go make us some coffee so I can avoid seeing you naked." She hurried out of the room.

She was gone so fast he didn't have time for a comeback. Not that he had one in mind. She'd progressed from an entertaining, sexy companion to a gorgeous woman who could strike him speechless.

20

Kendall was used to managing on her own, but Cheyenne certainly brightened up the place. Despite fantasizing about him for years, she'd never had a chance to give those fantasies a reality check. He could have had some habit she couldn't abide. Or vice-versa. She might have had some unconscious behavior that he'd find annoying.

Midway through their second day together, nothing had surfaced. He was easy to have around. Since he looked happy to be here, she must not wear on his nerves, either.

Over breakfast he'd made suggestions for projects they could tackle — fixing her wonky pasture gate and resetting a leaning post on the far side of her pasture fence. The gate had taken up most of the morning.

She was grateful for the repair. She'd put up with a sagging gate because fixing it took two pairs of hands. But when the second pair belonged to Cheyenne, a chore had become a sensual adventure.

Now that she'd felt his clever touch on her naked body, watching him expertly handling tools and wrestling the gate into place had sent shivers up her spine. And ideas spinning through her overheated brain.

After they cleaned up the lunch dishes, he hung up the dish towel and turned to her. "Ready to go take care of that fence post? I forgot to ask if you have a bag of cement."

"I do, but how about tackling that post project in the morning?"

He studied her, clearly trying to read between the lines. "No time like the present."

"And heaven knows I don't want Mischief and Mayhem escaping."

"I'm not too worried about that. They wouldn't go far, but—"

"How about this? It's a beautiful day. Let's take a nice long ride. Blow the cobwebs off those horses. Then we'll put them back in the barn and take care of the post tomorrow."

"Hm." His cheek dented with the hint of a smile. "Would this outing include strapping a rolled blanket to the back of one of our saddles?"

"Depends. Do you want to fool around before tonight's party or wait until after we get back?"

"Both."

"Right answer."

The light in his gaze changed from amused to electric. "Let me guess. A chapter in that book suggested doing it in the great outdoors?"

"Might have."

Heat flared in his eyes. "If you'll fetch the blanket I'll catch the horses."

"Then that's a yes?"

He laughed. "I've been doing my damnedest to dial it back, but passing up this invitation takes a stronger man than me." He grabbed his hat from the back of his chair. "See you down at the barn."

"Yippee!" She dashed to the linen closet where she kept spare blankets and chose a thick, sturdy quilt that she could throw in the washer later.

Then she made a quick trip to the bedroom and pocketed a condom. After filling a couple of stainless steel bottles with water, she headed for the barn, anticipation fizzing in her veins.

He came through the newly repaired gate leading both horses. She paused to drink in the sight of him — tall, broad-shouldered, his stride slightly bow-legged from years of riding. The setting she loved fit him perfectly.

But...he already had a house on land he owned at Rowdy Ranch. She clamped down on that train of thought and kept walking toward the barn. She was getting way ahead of herself.

He looked up and grinned. "That's quite a bedroll you have there. Whoever takes it will have a backrest."

"The book says not to skimp on the blanket. If it's too thin, that will impact whoever's on the bottom."

"Have you decided which of us that will be?"

"Not yet. Have you done it?"

He broke eye contact and led the horses to the hitching post. "A time or two."

"That's all?"

He glanced at her and smiled. "I'm dodging the question."

"Why?"

He busied himself tethering Mischief and Mayhem and didn't look at her. "When a guy still lives in his mom's house and his girlfriends are in the same situation, heading out into the woods is the answer."

"Oh. I suppose it would be." She deflated some. "Is it old hat to you, then?"

Leaving the hitching post, he walked over to her and laid his hands on her shoulders. "Nothing is old hat if I'm doing it with you. Doesn't matter how many times I've had sex outdoors. You never have, so that makes it special for me, too."

"What a lovely thing to say."

"It's the truth." He hesitated. "You know, I can't help wondering..." Then he shook his head. "Never mind. Let's tack up those horses."

"What are you wondering about?"

Gazing at her, he paused for a beat. "All right, but if the question's too personal, just say so and I'll drop it."

"I doubt I'll say that."

"Then...why didn't you experiment with sex when you were younger?"

Not too personal, but maybe too reveling. "Didn't appeal to me."

He nodded. "I'm guessing the high school guys turned you off. At that age, most of us are bulls in a china shop, at least for the first couple of years. It's a wonder the ladies put up with our clumsy behavior."

"There you go."

"But in the time since then, you haven't met anyone who... interested you?"

She shrugged. "I'm picky." Which was almost too much of a hint.

Squeezing her shoulders, he let go and took a deep breath. "And then your dad got sick. I can't picture you dating up a storm when you were worried about him. Time could easily slip by."

"Right."

"I just hope...and it's probably my oversized ego that makes me think this is even possible.... I just hope you haven't been saving yourself for..." He glanced up at the sky. "I feel like an idiot for saying it, but I hope you haven't been saving yourself for me."

Bingo. Should she confess? She'd have to eventually. But not now, when he didn't want it to be true.

If she hung in there, the day might come when he'd be thrilled to learn he'd been her only choice all along. That day wasn't here.

She needed to say something, though. If she stayed silent, he could draw the wrong conclusion. Or the right one. "Cheyenne, I respect you and I—"

"Right, right. Just as I thought, my ego put that idea in my head. The bachelor auction happened to come at a time when you were ready to take the next step."

"Yes, it did."

"And you bid on me because I was a known quantity."

Known quantity? The guy was an expert at selling himself short. "I've also had a crush on you for quite a while."

"I did know that. Makes sense that when you decided to venture into this space, you'd want someone who... well...."

"Turned me on?"

"Better for you to say it than me. But, yeah."

"And clearly you do. You've made moving into *this space* as you call it, a fabulous experience."

"Thank you." He chuckled. "It hasn't exactly been a hardship."

"I'm so glad to hear that. Shall we saddle up those ponies so we can continue the adventure?"

"Yes, ma'am."

As they headed into the barn to fetch the tack, she let out a quiet sigh of relief. His modesty had saved her from having to confess her deep and abiding love. He couldn't imagine he was special enough to inspire that kind of devotion. Someday she'd be able to tell him how special he was, especially to her.

21

Cheyenne tied the ginormous quilt behind Kendall's saddle. Took some doing, but eventually he'd secured it. "Biggest bedroll ever." He stepped back and gestured toward Mischief. "Your mount, milady."

"Thank you, kind sir." She hopped nimbly into the saddle and leaned back. "Great lumbar support. I could get used to this."

"I dare you to ride over to Rowdy Ranch with that big ol' blanket tied to your saddle."

"Do you mean that? Because I've never been able to resist—"

"Never mind." He grinned. "We'll get teased enough as it is. Besides, I vote we drive over there tonight instead of riding. Less trouble."

"I agree."

"I love riding, but you can't park a horse as easily as you can park a truck." He climbed aboard Mayhem.

"Not to mention coming home when it's cold." She glanced over at him and smiled. "How're you doing down there?"

"Smartass." The mare was about fifteen hands, at least a hand shorter than her son. But Kendall was a good ten inches shorter than he was, which evened them up some. He straightened his spine, which brought them eye-to-eye. "Does this horse make me look fat?"

She laughed. "I tried to give you Mischief."

"Wouldn't dream of it. Your horse, your custom saddle. I'm happy to ride your dad's mare. I can already tell she has a soft mouth."

"He doted on her." Kendall wheeled Mischief around and trotted past the barn toward the tree line. "Follow me."

He quickly caught up with her. "Didn't you have another horse at one point? I remember you riding over to the ranch and I don't think it was on this mare."

"It wasn't. I had Hank, a strawberry roan. Mom and Dad got him for me when I was in first grade."

"Okay. I remember you on that big horse." She'd been a towhead then, and so tiny for such a large animal. "You and Angie used to ride double."

"I loved him so much. He turned twenty-eight when I graduated. That's when Dad got Mayhem. He planned to breed her and give me the foal to raise, a hedge against the inevitable with Hank. But she had trouble getting pregnant."

"Horses are tricky."

"Yep. When Hank died, Dad was ready to give up on the idea and just get me another horse, but I loved the plan and said I'd wait. Mayhem finally conceived and the rest is history."

"I'll bet your dad was comforted that you'd have that foal, after all."

"He was. He paid for an ultrasound so he'd know if Mischief would be a colt or a filly, since... well, he didn't know if he'd be around for the birth." She sighed. "He almost made it."

And he'd raised a brave daughter who was carrying on without complaint. "I wish I'd been more help back then."

"You hugged me at the funeral. I sure appreciated that."

"I should've done more." He'd been a coward, afraid of giving her the wrong idea. Not even slightly noble.

"I understood, Cheyenne. I've made something of a pest of myself where you're concerned."

"You weren't so bad."

"Yes, I was. If you'd tried to be more comforting, who knows how I would have reacted? It was an emotional time. I might have made an inappropriate advance and embarrassed us both."

"After what's happened this past week, an inappropriate advance doesn't sound so bad."

"Oh, but it would have been. Timing is everything. I'm in a different place, now. I still miss my dad, but the worst of the grief is over."

"And so you're thinking of the future?"

"Exactly. First I had to prove to myself that I could run this ranch on my own. Which I have, if you don't count a sagging gate and a leaning fence post."

"Those don't count. Every ranch has something that needs to be fixed. Ask Sky and Buck about their to-do list. This place is in great shape. You've done a terrific job."

"Thank you. That means a lot coming from you."

"I admire your spirit, Sunshine. I don't think I've told you that, but I've thought it plenty of times since Friday."

"Now you're making me blush."

He glanced over, and sure enough, her cheeks were pink. "Looks good on you."

She met his gaze.

The heartfelt glow in her gray eyes filled him with longing. He wanted to hold her. And not let her go for a very long time.

Then she looked away. "I said we should blow the cobwebs off these horses, but we'll never do that trotting slowly along like a couple of greenhorns. Race you to the tree line!" And she took off.

Mayhem got a late start, but the mare wasn't about to be left in the dust. She lunged forward so abruptly he lost his seat and had to grab for his hat. By the time he was back in control, they were right on Mischief's heels.

Kendall glanced over her shoulder. "Nice riding!"

"It's not me. Mayhem's the one who refuses to be bested by her son."

Kendall laughed. "That's why I needed a head start. She's small, but she runs like the wind."

"So I see." Mayhem swerved to the right and put on a burst of speed that brought her neck-in-neck with Mischief. "Where's the finish line of this race?"

"That poplar sitting out by itself." Her voice was breathy. "Gives you enough time to pull up before you get to the dense forest."

"See you there!" He gave Mayhem a nudge with his heels. As if she needed it. She'd clearly had her eye on that poplar and knew exactly what it signified.

Lifting his hat in the air, he let out a whoop and leaned over her neck as she put on the afterburners. He looked back as the poplar flashed by. Mayhem had put a length between her and her son.

"Whoa, girl. Easy does it." He reined her in gently and put on his hat as she arched her neck and pranced in a circle, blowing through her nose. She acted like a thoroughbred who'd just won the Derby.

"God, that was awesome." Kendall rode over, her face alight. "She loves to race."

"Has Mischief ever beat her?"

"Nope. I don't think he cares enough. She puts her heart and soul into it." Kendall tilted her head toward a break in the trees. "We'll take that path to cool 'em off. She likes to lead, so go ahead."

He headed Mayhem toward the opening. "How far?"

"You'll know when you get there. So will she."

Mayhem snorted and bobbed her head as if she knew they were discussing her.

"This mare's loaded with personality."

"Today more than usual. Maybe you bring back memories of my dad. I know she misses him."

"She must if they were close."

The mare's velvet ears swiveled back.

He leaned down and stroked her sweaty neck. "Thanks for a great ride, girl."

She snorted again, her delicate hooves almost dancing along the path.

He turned in the saddle so he could see Kendall. "I'm gonna guess we're on the way to a favorite picnic spot."

"Not just a favorite picnic spot. My favorite place on the whole ranch."

"I'm honored." He faced forward again.

"I think you'll like it."

"If you do, I'm sure I will. Especially considering what we plan to—" Uh-oh. He hadn't come prepared. What a doofus. "Hey, Sunshine, I hate to tell you this, but I forgot to bring—"

"Got you covered, cowboy. Literally."

"I'm happy to hear it. And feeling pretty stupid. I totally forgot, and I'm supposed to be the experienced one around here."

"I threw you off your game by luring you away from your afternoon of hard labor to cavort in the woods."

"Cavort? Will we be playing naked hide-and-seek?"

"Hey, that's a thought."

"A terrible thought."

"A new twist would keep you from getting bored."

"It would keep me from having sex at all. Scampering around the woods buck naked is not my idea of foreplay. And FYI, there's not a chance in hell I'll be bored."

"Just kidding. I wouldn't have the nerve to do it. The other reason I brought a big blanket is so we can cover up if someone comes along."

"Would they?"

"I doubt it. I've made this trip hundreds of times with my dad and my friends. Recently I've been coming out here by myself with Mischief. Nobody's ever stumbled upon us. But I've never ridden out here prepared to strip down to nothing, either."

"We'll be fine. Are we close? All this talk has... well, let's just say the ride's less comfortable than it was."

"I'm getting a little squishy, myself."

He cleared his throat. "That info didn't help, Sunshine."

"The meadow's just around that curve in the path."

"Good." He kicked Mayhem into a trot and instantly regretted it. But the sun-washed meadow full of fragrant new grass and surrounded by sheltering pines helped ease his pain. He rode in and dismounted with relief. "Beautiful. Where do you usually put the horses?"

"Over here." She jumped down and led Mischief to one side of the meadow. "Mayhem's an old hand at being ground tied, especially in this location." She dropped the reins. "I've been working on Mischief. He's doing very well. And he won't leave his mom, so there's that."

"Excellent." He followed her over, dropped Mayhem's reins and gave her a pat. "She's a great horse."

"She likes you, too." Kendall untied the quilt from Mischief's saddle.

"How can you tell?"

"From her ears. They've been perked up the whole time and mostly turned in the direction of your voice. She also ran extra fast today. I think she was in high spirits."

"That makes two of us."

She turned toward him, the blanket in her arms. "Four of us, counting me and Mischief."

That made him smile. "Here, I'll take that." He relieved her of the bundle.

"I don't know if it's better to be over by the trees or over by that big rock, which—"

"Let's figure that out later." He put the rolled blanket at his feet.

"Later? Don't we need to find a spot so we can—"

"Eventually." Nudging his hat back, he drew her into his arms. "If I don't kiss you right this minute, I'm gonna explode."

She gazed up at him, her gray eyes shining. "That would put a crimp in our plans."

"That's why I mentioned it." Tucking her in close with one hand, he cupped her face with the other. "I've been holding off kissing you ever since we woke up together. No way I'd be able to stop with just a kiss."

Her breath caught. "Me, either."

"See, I knew that." He brushed his thumb over her soft cheek. "You'd fold just like me, and there goes the program of pacing ourselves. But the thing is, I've wanted to kiss you every second of this day."

"You have? Even when we worked on the gate?"

"Especially when we worked on the gate. There you were, right beside me, smelling like sugar cookies, looking like a lady who wanted to be kissed—"

"I did. Every. Single. Second."

"Then it's way past time." Heart pounding, he lowered his mouth to hers. Ahh, so good. So easy and natural. A perfect fit.

No woman had ever made him relax and heat up at the same time. Only this one. That should probably scare him. But he'd worry about that later. Right now, he was kissing Kendall. And nothing else mattered.

22

Another fantasy coming true. Kendall would have pinched herself except she was too busy unbuttoning Cheyenne's shirt and slipping her hands under his collar.

He had the warmest skin. And wow, could he kiss. Velvet lips, talented tongue. She wiggled closer, sliding her hips against his. His breath caught.

She did it again and he groaned. Yeah, baby. He was ready. Which made her ache like crazy. Only one way to take care of that.

She reached down and unfastened his belt. Might as well unbutton his jeans, too.

He lifted his head, his breathing unsteady. "Trying to tell me something?"

"Uh-huh. Are you getting the message?"

"Message received." Releasing her, he scooped up the blanket, wrapped an arm around her shoulders and started off.

"Did you pick out a spot?"

"Yes, ma'am." He stopped abruptly. "Right here."

"Why here?"

His laughter was ragged. "It's as far as I can walk in this condition."

"Then here it is." She trembled as she helped him spread out the quilt.

"I'm glad you went big." He toed off his boot and set it to one side.

"Me, too." She followed his lead and started to take off her boots.

"Hang on, Sunshine. Can I do that?" He set his other boot next to the first and walked over in his sock feet.

"Do what?"

"Undress your sweet self." He scooped her up in his arms.

The sudden move made her gasp.

"Sorry. Did I startle you?"

"Yes." She wrapped her arms around his neck. "But I like it."

His gaze softened. "I've had the urge to pick you up ever since... Friday night, I guess. Pick you up and carry you off to bed."

Sexy words. Thrilling words. "Why didn't you?"

"I didn't have that right. You'd never been with a man and hauling you in there would have been... just wrong. The first move had to be yours." He laid her gently on the blanket.

"Then thank goodness I made it."

"Thank goodness." Dropping to his knees, he braced a hand on either side of her head. Then he leaned down and kissed her, delving deep.

She cupped the back of his neck and opened to him, craving everything he had to offer.

The midday sun warmed her, but his kiss made her skin flush hot and her clothes became a nuisance she could do without.

As if he could read her mind, he shifted his weight to one hand and began unbuttoning her shirt. She wrenched the tails from the waistband of her jeans and started working from the bottom.

He lifted his mouth a fraction from hers. "Am I going too slow?"

"Yes, so I'm—"

"Maybe I need to switch things up."

"Good idea."

Reaching down, he unfastened her jeans and pulled down the zipper.

"Great. While you do that, I'll—" She gasped as he slipped his hand inside her panties. "What are... ohhhh." He had magic fingers. In no time he'd brought her to the brink.

He nibbled on her mouth as he continued his intimate caress. "Is this what you had in mind?"

She gulped as her climax hovered ever closer. "It'll do. For now."

"Good to know." He pushed deeper and pressed down with his thumb.

She came apart instantly. Arching into his knowing touch, she cried out as a flood of pleasure swept her along, carrying her to a release that rocked her from the roots of her hair to the tips of her toes.

He kept his fingers buried, stroking gently as the flow of sensual delight ebbed and her breathing slowed. Sliding his hand free, he dropped light kisses on her forehead, her cheeks, and finally her mouth. "Better?"

She took a deep breath and gazed up at him. "That was... a surprise."

He smiled. "But a nice one?"

"Oh, yes. Although it has to be torture for you."

"Torture?"

"Watching me enjoy myself when you need the very same thing."

"But it's not torture. I love watching your response. When I can give you something you need, that feels great."

"Well, thank you, because I was a little bit manic and now... not so much."

"So I can undress you and you won't care how long it takes?"

"You really want to do that?"

"It's one of my favorite things."

"Oh." New information. "I figured you'd want easy access. Then you can get right down to business."

"That's fun. But there's a reason folks wrap a gift." Pushing up on his elbow, he stroked his still-damp fingers over the hollow in her throat. "It builds anticipation."

"You've already seen the gift."

"True." He undid the last few buttons of her shirt. "But was I taking the time to really look at you? I don't think so." As he opened her shirt, his focus moved downward, pausing at her white cotton bra. "Now that's unexpected."

"What?"

"This." He flipped the front catch.

Her heart beat faster. Being undressed by Cheyenne was a turn-on for her, too. Who knew?

He gazed into her eyes as he pushed the bra aside. "I figured you for having the type that fastens in the back."

"I had one like this... yesterday." Her words came out in a breathless murmur. He'd just given her a powerful climax and it wasn't enough.

"See? I didn't notice. You whipped it off so fast." He cupped her breast in his warm, strong hand.

"Easy access." She could barely speak.

The corners of his mouth tipped up. "Sexy, too." Once again his attention drifted downward. "So pretty, Sunshine." He squeezed gently. "I love looking at you."

She gripped the quilt with both hands. "I... want you again."

"I can tell." Dipping his head, he closed his mouth over her aching nipple and began to suck.

She gasped as her core tightened. She couldn't possibly... oh, yes, she could. Panting, helpless before the onslaught, she rode the wild waves of another glorious orgasm.

"Unbelievable." She gulped for air.

His soft chuckle cooled her moist skin. "Not to me."

"I didn't know."

"Like I said, you're a gift." Changing his position, he started tugging off her jeans.

She tried to help by lifting her hips. Nope. "I'm a ragdoll. You're on your own."

"No worries." He pulled them off, taking her panties with them.

And her socks. Cool air touched the soles of her feet. She gazed up, squinting a little as the breeze moved the top branches of the pine that was blocking the sun. Her shirt still covered her arms, but otherwise she was lying naked under a blue Montana sky.

And she didn't care. Two excellent orgasms had cancelled any remaining modesty.

"You look amazing."

She turned her head. He stood a couple of feet away, unbuttoning his shirt. Her body stirred. "I'd undress you if I had the energy."

"Good thing you don't. I couldn't handle it." He let his shirt drop and unzipped his jeans.

"I believe you." She admired the jut of his cock as he shoved off his jeans and briefs. Great angle. Her core responded. Again. Evidently she wasn't finished, after all. "I didn't know being undressed would get me so hot."

He just smiled.

"You did, though, didn't you?"

"I had a pretty good idea, but I could have been wrong." He leaned down, picked up something lying on the quilt and ripped open the small package.

"You found it."

"Yes, ma'am." After rolling on the condom, he dropped to his knees beside her, chest heaving. He blocked another flash of sunlight as he leaned in to give her a sweet, undemanding kiss. Then he lifted his head. "I think we've settled who'll be on top."

"I think so."

His gaze locked with hers, he moved into position, his palms flattened against the quilt, his hips slowly lowering. "I promise you don't have to do much of anything. I'll—"

"This might shock you, but I'm fired up again." Smoothing her hands down his muscular back, she gripped his firm backside.

His breath caught. "You're incredible, Sunshine."

"You're not so bad, yourself, cowboy." She urged him lower, rising slightly to meet his first thrust.

His eyes darkened. The he plunged deep.

She sucked in air.

"Okay?"

"More than okay. This is... the best."

Warmth filled his expression. "For me, too." He swallowed. "For me, too." And he began to thrust, slowly at first, then faster.

She rose to meet him, her fingers pressing into his glutes as they tightened and released, tightened and released. Through it all, he kept his attention on her, his face wearing that same tender expression.

He was probably waiting for her, wanting her to come first. She let go gladly. He smiled and stroked even faster until, with a hoarse cry, he pushed home and tumbled into the whirling joy of release.

When he stayed braced above her, his arms taut, she wrapped him in a bear hug. "Come down here. Lie with me."

"I'm heavy."

"I'm sturdy."

"No question, but—"

"Quit arguing, Cheyenne. I want to feel your manly chest against my tatas."

He grinned and lowered himself to his forearms. "How's that?"

"More."

"You asked for it." He sank down, giving her his full weight and resting his head on her shoulder. "Can you breathe?"

"Sure." She tested it. "Well, not exactly."

"Told you." He used his forearms for support so he could settle down without crushing her. "I'll bet I weigh twice as much as—" He stopped talking and lifted his head. "I hear something."

She went very still. "Some*thing* or some*body*?" Maybe she wasn't so comfy-cozy about her nakedness, after al.

"Don't know. There's a rustling in the bushes. Listen."

Sure enough, the underbrush was being disturbed. Her heart pumped faster. "Can you see anything?"

"No, I… wait… yes. Over to the left, there's a face."

"Grab the edges of the blanket. Cover us up."

"Shh. You'll scare it."

"It?" A critter, not a person. Maybe Bigfoot.

He dropped his voice to a low murmur. "Turn your head slowly. You should be able to see it, too."

Her neck popped as she adjusted her position She whispered a quick *sorry*.

"No worries. It's still there."

At last her cheek rested on the quilt. She peered into the leafy shadows. Something stared back at her. Something with pointy ears, dark eyes and a long nose. The swift fox.

"See it?"

"Uh-huh." She kept her voice low. "Do you think it's been there the whole time?"

"No idea."

"But this was the first you heard anything moving?"

"Until this minute I was incapable of hearing anything moving. I would've been deaf to a charging grizzly."

"That's not comforting. Although the horses would have alerted us to a bear."

"Not sure I would have heard the horses, either."

"Why do you suppose it's just sitting there watching us?"

"Might have a den on the far side of that big rock. We could be in its way."

"Can you reach your phone?"

He chuckled. "*No*. Can you?"

"Of course not." She sighed. "I'll just have to report the sighting without photographic evidence."

He turned his head to gaze at her, his blue eyes sparkling. "Can't wait to read that report, Sunshine."

23

Cheyenne wanted nothing more than to stay in the meadow with Kendall until the stars came out and the moon rose. But they had horses to tend and chickens to tuck in for the night. Hanging out in the meadow wouldn't work for the little fox, either, who probably had made a home somewhere nearby.

Kendall promised they'd come back soon. The fox wouldn't be happy about that, and Cheyenne wasn't convinced it was a good idea for the humans, either. The longer they kept this situation going, the tougher it would be to part ways.

Sharing the evening barn chores and helping bed down those chickens drove home the point. He was enjoying himself too much. He'd be wise to dial it back.

After taking care of the animals, they had very little time to get ready for his mom's party. Turned out it didn't matter. A shower and a change of clothes did the trick for Kendall. No makeup, no fussing with her hair.

Her jeans had a little bling on the back pockets, so not the ones she'd wear for mucking out stalls. Likewise her purple shirt had a design embroidered on the yoke, clearly an outfit for special occasions. She wore her dancing boots, the ones she'd had on Friday night at the Buffalo.

He'd never seen a prettier woman, and he told her so as they each grabbed a jacket for later and headed toward the front door.

"Thank you." She gave him a dimpled smile. Then she plucked her keys from a hook on the wall. "I'll drive."

He already had his keys in his pocket. "That's okay. I'll take us."

"But you've done all the driving so far. You brought me home Friday night and you took me into town to get the electric fence supplies. The trip to Rowdy Ranch is too short to make us even, but it's absolutely my turn."

"I didn't know we were taking turns." And she'd thrown him off his game. He traded driving chores with his family all the time, but in a relationship with a woman, he'd always taken his truck.

"It just makes sense, since we each have a vehicle."

He took his hat from the rack by the door and brushed a speck of lint from the crown before meeting her gaze. "Do you want to drive?"

"I do, actually. Is that a problem?"

"Of course not. I'm just used to driving when I go somewhere with a lady I'm involved with."

She smiled. "I figured that's why you were discombobulated. It's lovely that you want to drive me everywhere, but it's... well, old-fashioned."

He blinked. "I don't care."

"But I do."

"What about opening the door for you? That's old-fashioned and you don't seem to mind."

"I don't mind at all. I appreciate the courtesy."

"Driving you is also a courtesy."

"It can be if someone can't or doesn't want to drive. But I like it. And I'm good at it."

"I'm sure you are, but—"

"When Lucky and I go dancing at the Buffalo, we trade off."

"But my little brother is just a friend, whereas I'm... I mean, we're...." He couldn't figure out how to end the sentence, so he gave up.

"I don't know how to describe us, either. We're not exactly dating."

"But we're not like you and Lucky."

"God, no." She laughed again. "I would never... well, he's a sweetheart, but he's never given me butterflies. Not even once."

And wasn't he extremely happy to hear it? Not a good sign. "Let's just say we're in a relationship."

"That works. It also makes my point. Angie's never let a guy she's in a relationship with become the de facto driver. I think that's an excellent policy."

"Hm." Interesting concept. Obviously she planned to stand her ground. She might have a huge crush on him, but that didn't mean she'd let him do whatever he wanted. He liked that. A lot. "It'll be my pleasure to ride shotgun."

Her answering smile was a knockout. "Wonderful."

That happy smile filled him with so much joy he was light-headed as he took the keys out of his pocket and hung them where hers had been. Then he put on his hat and opened the door for her. "Shall we go?"

"Yes." She sailed through like royalty.

He followed her out and took her hand as they went down the steps. "Are you going to help me into your truck, too?"

She giggled. "I should, shouldn't I?"

"Please don't. How about if I help you into the driver's seat? Can we make that the compromise?"

"Sure, why not? This is all new territory for me."

"It's new territory for me, too. No woman has ever objected to me being the de facto driver."

"Maybe they just don't like to drive. But Angie and I both do. We flip a coin whenever we go somewhere together."

"I get that, but when I take a woman out, I feel like I should drive."

"Was it a date when we went to buy the fence?"

"No, but—"

"And technically, you're not taking me out tonight. We're both invited to this party and we're going together, but you didn't ask me out. Clint stopped by and asked us to come."

"I have a hunch you were in debate class in high school."

"How'd you know?"

"You make your case the way my sister would. She was in debate." He opened the driver's door and helped her into the truck. Weird. So was walking around and getting in on the other side.

He closed the door and buckled up. "We should go on a date."

She grinned. "Are you asking or telling?"

"Sorry. I'm asking. Would you like to go to the Buffalo with me tomorrow night for dinner and dancing?" *Way to dial it back, dude.*

"I would love to." She backed the truck out, put it in gear and pulled forward onto the dirt road leading out of her place.

"Would it bother you if I drove?"

She chuckled. "No, it wouldn't. Your idea, your truck. But if I ask you out, then it's my turn."

"Okay." He settled back in the seat. "Didn't the Wagon Train High debate team win a state championship?"

"Senior year. We were invincible."

"You still are, Sunshine." He glanced at her. Nice view. He'd never studied her profile before. Now he had the perfect opportunity.

She had long lashes, something that wasn't obvious because she didn't use mascara. He liked the way the tip of her nose tilted up a little. A natural blush spread over her cheeks and deepened by the second.

She swallowed. "Driving with you in the truck is harder than I thought it would be."

"Oh?" He pretended innocence. "Why's that?"

"You're staring at me."

"I know. I'm free to do that now that I'm a passenger."

"You're getting me hot."

"Now you know how I feel when I'm driving and you're looking at me."

"Oh." She sighed. "I guess I do that, huh?"

"I'm not complaining. But sometimes it's a challenge to keep my attention on the road."

"I understand that, now."

"Do you want me to stop looking at you?"

"No. I'll just learn how to handle it, like you do."

He smiled. "Right answer."

"We're almost there, anyway. I just realized that I didn't bring anything to the party."

"You brought me."

"That was a given. But I could have brought something like a cheese dip. The cookies are almost gone, but if I'd thought of it, I could have baked a pie. Everybody likes my pies."

"And when would you have baked that pie?"

She took a moment to answer. "Excellent question. Sex takes up time, doesn't it?"

"Yes, but most folks don't mind, especially if it's good sex." She was hilarious. He couldn't resist teasing her. "Given the choice between having good sex and baking a pie, I'm thinking—"

"Okay, okay, I'm glad I had sex with you today instead of baking a pie." She giggled. "Maybe I should explain that's why we're arriving empty-handed."

He opened his mouth, ready to dare her to say that. Then he closed it again. Daring Kendall to do something wasn't a wise move unless he was prepared for the consequences.

"Don't worry, Cheyenne. I won't really say it." She pulled into a parking space.

"You can say anything you want."

"I know, but I saw the look on Clint's face when he came by your house yesterday. You're in for some teasing tonight."

"I can take it."

"But I'm going to try very hard not to make it worse. For example, let's agree to separate once we're in there so neither of us looks clingy."

"Good idea." A twinge of disappointment told him he'd be the one most likely to cling. Yeah, he was a needy Ned.

He blamed the looming expiration date on this setup. He'd served his purpose and she was ready to launch into dating. She even had her first rule in place. No de facto drivers.

But she wasn't part of the singles scene yet. "Are you still okay with leaving early?"

"Sure am. Just come get me when you're ready to go."

"What if you're not ready to go? Should we have a signal for that?"

"We don't need one. If you want to leave because you can't wait to get me into bed, I'll be happy to say my goodbyes."

That sent a message straight to his privates. "Alrighty, then." He glanced over as Clint pulled up right next to them. His twin did a double-take. Cheyenne climbed out, careful not to bump doors with Clint.

"Something wrong with your truck, bro?"

"No, I—"

"He was man enough to ride over with me when I announced I wanted to drive." Kendall rounded the back of the truck.

She must have hopped out immediately, which she should. Helping her into the driver's side worked. Expecting her to sit there until he came around to help her out was…exactly what he normally expected ladies to do. Huh.

Clint tipped his hat. "Evening, Kendall. Did my brother mention that riding shotgun is a departure from his normal behavior?"

"Yes, he did. But he was willing to be flexible."

"She's in favor of our sister's policy," Cheyenne said.

"Which one? She has several."

"The transportation policy. Any guy she dates will not become the de facto driver."

Clint scratched his chin. "I wasn't aware of that policy. But then, since she almost never brings her boyfriends around, we wouldn't know if he's the de facto driver or not."

"He wouldn't be." Kendall tucked her jacket over her arm. "If the guy insists on doing all the driving, she won't date him."

"Another litmus test. I pity the poor saps, but I'm glad she's picky." He paused. "And you've adopted this driving policy of hers?"

"I have."

"If Cheyenne had refused to ride over here with you, would it have been curtains for him?"

She smiled. "Come on, Clint. Can you picture him refusing?"

"Hey, you two. I'm right here."

"Now that you mention it, I can't." Clint faced him, his eyes sparkling. "I do believe she's got your number, bro."

He had no comeback. His twin had nailed it. Kendall knew him well, maybe even better than he knew himself.

24

Earlier in the year, Desiree had given Kendall a peek at Rowdy Roost, the game room and saloon she'd added to her ever-changing ranch house. But that visit had been during the day.

Tonight the ruby vintage lights glowed, lively games of pool and darts were in progress, and a George Strait song poured from a top-of-the-line sound system. The intricately carved mirrored bar, complete with leather stools mounted on swiveling bases, rivaled the one at the Buffalo. Rance mixed drinks decked out in a brocade vest and string-tie outfit that made him look like a riverboat gambler.

Clint had walked in with Kendall and Cheyenne, but then he excused himself to go play pool.

"It's an amazing place. So much to look at." Kendall pointed to the faux balcony along one wall. "I almost believe there's a second story up there with rooms for rent."

"Mom would have loved to create that scenario for our rooms when we were little, but she didn't have the money. She can't justify it now that we've all moved out, so she settled for a good fake."

"I don't remember seeing the Rowdy Roost sign over the bar when I was here in January. Did Bret and Gil make it?"

"Yes, ma'am. Mom was all set to order a wooden sign and they offered to make one out of horseshoes."

"That's so much better. They must be doing well. I see their designs everywhere."

"Yep. Now the ironworks business brings in more than shoeing horses. Folks love their—"

"Hey, you guys snuck in on me." Angie came over, all smiles.

"I needed a minute to absorb all this wonderfulness." Kendall swept an arm around the room. "It looked great in the daylight, but it really shines at night."

"That it does. So, what have you two been up to today?"

Cheyenne coughed and cleared his throat. "We, uh—"

"Fixed the pasture gate." Kendall jumped in. She didn't care whether Angie found out about their adventure in the meadow, but she'd rather not start the conversation with that subject.

"Yay! I've been meaning to help you with that for a long time." She turned toward Cheyenne. "Well done, big brother. I heard about the electric fence you and Kendall installed yesterday. If you decide to give up firefighting, you can come work for me."

He chuckled. "Thanks, sis. I'll keep it in mind."

"Seriously, I might need to hire some help. Now that spring is here, the Wagon Train Handywoman is going gangbusters. I can't keep up with the work."

"Kendall's pretty handy."

"Why, thank you." She gave him a quick smile.

"I know she is," Angie said. "We had fun building the chicken coop."

"Yeah, that was a blast." Kendall gazed at her friend as Cheyenne's comment took hold. "Want to hire me?"

Angie's eyes widened. "I'd love to! Do you have the time?"

"You know what? I do. I used to think managing the ranch was a full-time job, but it's not. I have more free hours in the day than I realized." She didn't dare look at Cheyenne, who'd been responsible for demonstrating how much spare time she had.

"This is the best news. Are you sure? Because if you mean it, I'd like you to start next week."

"I mean it. And next week sounds good to me." She grinned at Cheyenne. "Thanks for making that comment about me being handy. Now I have a job."

"I'm glad I said something." He glanced at her, warmth lighting his blue eyes. "You'll be great at this."

Her breath caught. In the past few days, his expression had telegraphed lust plenty of times. By now she knew that look well. This was different. The glow in his eyes and his tender smile had nothing to do with sex. Which left... she was afraid to put a name to it. The stakes were too high.

"She'll be awesome." Angie was studying her brother. "I can't believe I didn't think of—"

"Hey, Ange." Beau came over holding a fistful of darts. "Are we playing or— hey, Kendall and Cheyenne! Wanna play darts? Jess and I challenged Angie and Lucky, but we can make it a three-way."

"I'm giving my spot to Kendall," Angie said. "Lucky would much rather have her than me. The two of them can annihilate any competition."

Beau's eyebrows lifted. "Are you nuts? Why would you let two power players be on the same team?"

"Because they're fun to watch."

"And you want me to get my ass kicked. Here's a better plan. You stick with Lucky and let Kendall team up with Cheyenne. That way we don't break up our newly minted couple."

"Beau." Angie gave him the stink-eye.

"Am I wrong? They came in together and Cheyenne keeps giving Kendall mushy looks, so I think it's fair to say—"

"Thanks for the invite," Cheyenne said, "but I promised Clint I'd shoot pool with him. See y'all later." Tipping his hat, he gave Kendall a wink and ambled away.

"I'll add a wink to my premise that they are, indeed, a couple." Beau smiled. "I know what I know."

"And I know you're a troublemaker." Angie swatted him on the arm. "Sorry, Kendall. I tried to set some guidelines for this crew, but—"

"It's okay." She was still mentally fanning herself after that sexy wink. "We knew we'd be in for it. The timing guaranteed that everyone would be curious about— wait, was the party scheduled tonight on purpose?"

"I swear it wasn't." Angie turned as Jess came over. "Back me up, here. Kendall just asked if we organized this party so we could get the scoop on her and Cheyenne."

Jess laughed. "That's just a bonus. It's nuts trying to find a time everyone can be here. My dad was supposed to come, but he got held up at the paper."

"We almost didn't make it, ourselves," Beau said. "The hair salon was holding Jess captive. I had to ride in and rescue her before they plucked her bald-headed."

"I like the new look," Kendall said. "Suits you."

"Beau didn't want me to have it cut this short." She ran her fingers through her sassy red curls. "You're the one who inspired me. I want something easy for when little Maverick makes her appearance."

"You'll love it. I keep trying to sell Angie on short hair."

"And I keep holding out."

"So back to the issue on the table." Beau held his darts in the air. "Who's playing?"

"I will," Kendall said. "But I'd like to get a drink from our friendly bartender first."

"Absolutely." Angie held up her empty glass. "And I need a refresh on mine."

"C'mon, Jess." Beau put an arm around his wife's shoulders. "Let's you and me sneak in some practice. And brush up on our trash talk. That might be all that saves us." He hugged her close as they walked away.

Angie let out a happy sigh. "So sweet."

"I know."

"And speaking of that." She started toward the bar. "I think..." She leaned closer and lowered her voice. "I think Cheyenne's falling for you."

"You do?" That news jacked up her pulse rate. "How can you tell?"

"Do you remember his pet rabbit?"

"The one that died the day of his prom?"

"Yes."

"I remember, but what's a rabbit got to do with—"

"I'll get to that." She grinned. "Never could teach that bunny to use a litter box. Even after five years, he'd still leave deposits all over the house." She slid onto a bar stool. "Rance, do you remember Cheyenne's rabbit?"

"Hippity Hoppity Poopity?" He threw a bar towel over his shoulder as he approached. "Sure do. Dramatic death scene. One minute he was fine, the next he was gone. I thought for sure Cheyenne would stay home from that prom."

"He should have," Angie said.

"But he wouldn't have wanted to disappoint his date." Kendall had fantasized what it would have been like to be that girl and how she'd comfort him for his loss. Typical thirteen-year-old, she'd soaked up the drama of Hippity's passing and Cheyenne's grief.

"Yeah, his precious date." Angie made a face.

"Are you ladies here to talk rabbits and prom dates or get drinks?"

"Get drinks." Angie handed over her glass. "Just a refill on my wine, please."

"Easy-peasy. Kendall, what about you?"

"Do you have any of that hard cider from Apple Grove?"

"I do." He handed Angie her wine glass and turned to open the small refrigerator behind him. "Ever since Mom revisited her old hometown, she likes to keep some on hand." He popped the top. "Want a glass?"

"No, thanks. The bottle's fine. Love the Old West vibe you have going on, Rance."

"Mom's idea, but it turns out I look good in a vest, so I'm okay with it."

Angie rolled her eyes. "Every guy looks good in a vest."

"Let me rephrase. I don't just look good in a vest, I look hot." He picked up a cocktail shaker and flipped it in the air. "Which I so am."

Angie groaned and tugged Kendall away from the bar. "Let's go play darts."

"Hang on." She paused and glanced back. Rance had moved to the other end of the bar and was talking with Marybeth. "You never made the connection between Hippity and Cheyenne falling for me."

"Ah, you're right. The point is, he was totally in love with that critter. It was a selfless, pure kind of love. He only wanted the best for Hippity. I've never seen him look at a girlfriend that way, and I've been watching. But after we picked up on his comment and decided to work together, he looked at you that way."

"Like I was his pet rabbit?"

"No, of course not. I'm just saying you should keep being your own wonderful self, and eventually he'll figure out he can't live without you."

"And bonus, I have a longer projected life span than a rabbit."

Angie smiled. "Yeah, there's that. Oh, here comes Mom."

"Welcome to Rowdy Roost." Desiree gave Kendall a hug.

"It's even more incredible at night."

Desiree glanced around, clearly a proud mom. "Especially when the gang's all here, as they say. Well, we're missing Jess's dad, but otherwise it's a full house." She beamed at Kendall. "How's it going over at the A-Plus?"

"Good, I guess. Angie claims that Cheyenne looks at me the same way he used to look at his rabbit Hippity."

"Well, he was crazy about that bunny." Her eyes sparkled with laughter. "Let's take that as a positive sign."

"I plan to."

"But I noticed you're with Angie and he's over there playing pool. Are you upset with each other?"

"Not at all. We agreed we'd do our own thing during the party."

"To cut down on the teasing?"

"Right."

"Seems like you're already operating as a team, then."

"I guess we are."

"Cheyenne's a great team player." Desiree glanced over at the pool table where he and Clint had taken on Marsh and Bret.

"That's one of the many things I love about him."

"So do I, although sometimes he takes it too far."

"How is that even possible?"

"I can't think of anything specific right now, but—"

"Oh, I can," Angie said. "That's the other part of the rabbit story I didn't tell you. He didn't want to go to the prom but he made himself do it. The next morning he was really down, worse than the day before."

"I remember," Desiree said. "I thought it might be a delayed reaction."

"I had a hunch it had something to do with the prom and I finally wormed it out of him. That nasty girl he'd invited spent the evening making jokes about his dead bunny rabbit."

"What?" Desiree's gaze snapped with anger. "You never told me that."

"I didn't tell anyone. Cheyenne begged me not to. He didn't want any of us, including me, cooking up ways to get even with her. And boy, did I have some cool plans for making that girl regret the day she was born."

"I would have been right there with you," Kendall said. "Is she still in town?"

Angie smiled. "I'm not sure, but I'll bet we could find out."

"Take it easy, girls. She and her family moved that summer, although Cheyenne broke up with her right after prom. Now I know why."

"But he just sucked it up through all those prom activities." Kendall sighed. "That must have been hell."

"Yep, that's my big brother. He didn't want to cast a pall over everyone's prom night or take a chance on ruining hers."

"I promise not to put him through hell while he's at my place."

"I'm sure you won't." Desiree met her gaze. "Listen, this is absolutely none of my business, but..."

"What?"

"The thing is, Cheyenne's never lived with anyone he's dated."

"He told me."

"Naturally, I can't help wondering if... well, is this temporary? Or..."

"The truth is, I don't know."

"I see."

"But I will keep you posted."

"Thanks." Desiree smiled. "You seem to be good for each other."

"I think we are." They weren't just good for each other. They were perfect. She just had to wait for Cheyenne to figure that out.

25

It was a great party. Shooting pool with his brothers, Cheyenne caught up on the latest from Marsh. Big surprise, his best friend Ella was engaged. They'd been buddies since grade school, and Cheyenne had always wondered if they'd end up together. They'd sworn it would never happen.

Evidently that was true if Ella was marrying someone else. Marsh had volunteered to help with wedding plans, so he must be cool with the matchup. Since the wedding was in August, only three months away, booking a venue for the ceremony and a band for the reception would take some fancy footwork.

Cheyenne kept an eye on the time as he estimated when he and Kendall could leave without causing a fuss. Not yet, but soon. Turning his pool cue over to Clint, he took a break to fetch more goodies from the buffet. He'd just loaded his plate when Sky came over wearing his big-brother expression.

He didn't bother to pick up a plate. "Got a minute?"

"Sure. You should grab some of those cheese puffs. Marybeth just brought in a fresh batch."

"Good idea. Believe I will." Sky put some cheese puffs and half of a chicken-salad sandwich on a plate. "You working on a beer?"

"Finished one a while ago."

"Then let's go hit up Rance for a couple of cold ones."

"Okay." Cheyenne had to smile. The party had been in progress for almost two hours. Sky had likely been appointed by the others to gather info and possibly ladle out some advice.

Once they had their beer, Sky gestured toward one of the small tables spaced along the wall. "Might as well take a load off."

"You're funny."

"I am?" Sky's gaze was steady.

"You didn't have to go through all this." He took one of the two chairs. "You could have just pulled me aside and asked me what was going on with Kendall."

Sky chuckled. "That lacks finesse." He took his seat on the other side of the table.

"Quicker, though."

"You got somewhere you need to be?" Amusement gleamed in his eyes.

"Nicely played, and yes, I do."

"Everybody has noticed, by the way. They figure you'll make your exit with Kendall any time, now. They told me to strike before the iron gets any hotter. So to speak." He took a sip of his beer.

"What do you want to know?"

"Your end game. That's assuming you have one. Mom asked Kendall if there was a plan, and she had no answer." He drank some more beer.

"That's interesting, because how this goes is mostly up to her."

"How so?"

"We've talked about her dating other guys, and she seems perfectly willing to do that." His gut clenched. "Whenever she's ready, I'll step out of the picture."

"Mom didn't get the impression that would happen anytime soon. She thinks Kendall's happy with things as they are." He took a big bite of his sandwich.

"Even if she is, that doesn't mean she's planning to stay put." He rolled his shoulders, trying to ease a slight ache. "She's a smart lady. She knows moving on is the right thing for her."

His brother chewed slowly and swallowed. "I wish you could see yourself. Your jaw's so tight you're gonna need Doc Bradbury to repair some cracked molars."

Leaning back in his chair, Cheyenne forced himself to take a deep breath and gulp down some beer. "You're right. I've let myself get invested. I—"

"Invested? Is that what they call it now? Back when I was your age, we had a simpler term. Less business-like."

"Don't push it, Sky. Yeah, she's terrific. But I'm not stupid enough to fall for her. That would be selfish. She started this process late and she has come catching up to do. I won't interfere with that."

"You say you've discussed this?"

"We have."

"And she's on the same page?"

"Why wouldn't she be? Nobody ends up sticking with their first. Not these days."

"I wouldn't say *nobody*."

"But you have to admit it's rare."

"I haven't exactly taken a poll."

"Look at the people in this room. Not a one of us fits in that category."

"You can't be sure about Buck and Marybeth."

"True. Why don't you go ask? Buck's right over there."

"No, thanks." Sky shuddered. "Sorry I brought it up. As far as I'm concerned, they've never had sex. Since they don't have kids, there's no proof they ever did."

"Coward."

"Yessir."

"Anyway, the rest of us prove my point. How can you possibly know someone's right for you when you have no frame of reference? Kendall only has me."

"But you have a frame of reference, bro. You clearly hate the idea of her being with another man. What if you've finally found—"

"Never mind." He chugged more beer.

"Admit it. You love her."

He put down the bottle and glared at his brother. "I can't."

"But—"

"Drop it, Sky. Please. Maybe I should have another talk with her and make sure we're thinking alike. You've made me aware of a possible misunderstanding. I'll clear that up."

"I would definitely advise more discussion. Judging from what mom said, Kendall—"

"Of course she'd give mom a vague answer. She'd hardly tell my devoted mother that next week she's kicking me out so she can play the field."

"I suppose not." Sky hesitated. "Do you think that's her plan?"

He shrugged, enduring the pain slicing through his chest like a chainsaw. "Could be. For all I know she's worried about hurting my feelings. If that's the case, I'll find out and set her straight."

"Good."

"Are we done, then? Because if we are, I'll see if Kendall's ready to call it a night."

"We're done. Once again, my timing was impeccable." He glanced at Cheyenne's untouched plate. "Are you going to eat that?"

"I thought so, but now I—"

"Feel the urge to leave so you and Kendall can have a talk?"

"Something like that."

"Listen, you really need to discuss things. Don't let sex get in the way."

"Spoken like a man who doesn't have these issues anymore."

"That's how much you know. Anyway, if you're not going to eat that food, I'll take it. I'd hate to see any of MaryBeth's efforts go to waste."

"Be my guest." He pushed the plate across the table and stood. "I'll go find Kendall." He started to walk away and paused. His brother had spoken out of loving concern. He turned back. "Thanks, Sky."

He smiled. "Anytime."

Cheyenne returned the smile and went looking for Kendall. He really was grateful to Sky and the rest of the family. They cared enough to be nosy.

Their questions were justified since abruptly moving in with Kendall wasn't like him at all. She was sailing through uncharted waters, but so was he.

In hindsight, his impulsive decision to stay at her place didn't make much sense, even to him. He could have enjoyed sex with her without turning it into an extended sleepover. But he didn't regret doing it, no matter how everything turned out. They were together now, and that was all that mattered.

Finding her in the crowd was easy, even though she was short and mostly hidden by his tall family. All he had to do was listen. Following the musical sound of her voice and the happy lilt of her laughter took him right to her.

In designing the game room, his mom had asked the carpenters to inlay an eight-by-eight-foot checkerboard in the floor. A local woodworker had created checkers the size of dinner plates.

Kendall was facing off against Gil and she had him cornered. His dark hair stuck out in all directions, a sign he'd been scrubbing his fingers through it. Kendall looked cool as a cucumber.

After Gil took the only move he had, Kendall picked up her stack of two, made three jumps and cleared the board. Cheyenne cheered along with everyone else.

Gil laughed, threw up his hands and walked over to give Kendall a hug. "Good game. One more?"

"Well..." Her gaze swept the group and settled on him.

Her smile was subtle. Maybe no one else caught it, but it arrowed straight into his rapidly beating heart.

She turned back to Gil. "Not tonight, I'm afraid. I'm ready to pack it in. Maybe we can do this again sometime soon, though."

"Count on it." His mom's face glowed with happiness. "C'mon, Gil." She started moving the stacked checkers back on the board. "Show me what you've got."

"Woo-hoo!" Angie stepped in to help. "Mom's playing. She's tough competition, Gil."

"I'm well aware."

Kendall came over to stand beside Cheyenne. "I'll bet she is good."

"Want to stay and watch?"

She glanced up at him, a gleam in her eyes. Lowering her voice, she leaned closer. "I'm ready to hit the hay."

Heat sluiced through his veins. "That's all I need to know." He raised his voice. "We're taking off. Great party, Mom."

"Thanks, son." She paused, a checker in each hand, and looked him in the eye. "Take care, okay?"

"I will." He slipped an arm around Kendall's waist. "Let's go, champ."

"I was lucky." She mirrored his action, wrapping her arm around him as they walked out.

"Don't give me that. You have skills."

"Played a ton of games with my dad." She dropped her voice to a murmur. "Do you think they're all watching us leave?"

"Could be."

"Was Sky giving you the third degree a while ago?"

"He just wants to make sure you and I are in agreement."

"About what?"

"That this thing between us isn't the end-all and be-all. That you plan to explore your options."

"I totally believe in exploring my options."

That got him right in the solar plexus. "Glad to hear it." *Not.* But it was exactly how she should be thinking.

"Let's go home and explore some options right now."

"My thoughts, exactly." Home. Did she realize she'd used that word? Whether she did or not, it resonated with him. In a good way. Sky's words rattled around in his brain. *You love her.*

Riding in the passenger seat still wasn't his favorite, but she navigated country roads like the competent country girl she was. He had no complaints, only a slight dent in his precious ego.

They made small talk on the way back, but once they were inside the house, all talk ceased.

They were naked and rolling around in her bed in record time.

"I thought we'd never get here." Her breathless words stoked the fire.

"But we did." Quickly rolling on a condom, he sank into her warmth with a groan of relief. "I love this." *I love you.*

"Me, too." She hooked her legs around his. "I can't imagine anything better."

Raising his head, he looked into her beautiful eyes. He could tell her a little bit of the truth. "Neither can I."

"You mean that?"

"Yes, ma'am." And then he loved her as thoroughly as he knew how. She believed in exploring her options. Which meant someday she would be gone.

She gave as good as she got, introducing sexy moves that drove him crazy. And she managed to delay her climax... somehow.

Panting, he finally asked her. "Are you holding back on purpose?"

She arched into his next thrust. "If you can, I can. I'm waiting for you."

"Seriously?" He pushed deep.

"Seriously. Give up?"

"Yes." He pumped faster.

"Then here goes." She surrendered, coming apart in his arms.

Honoring their unspoken agreement, he let go, his release wringing a cry from the depths of his aching heart. *Sunshine.*

26

Her sweet lover was troubled. Kendall could see it in his eyes, feel it in his touch, hear it in his voice, especially when he called out to her at the moment of release. But she hadn't broached the subject of his anxious state of mind.

Instead, she'd cuddled with him while they'd talked about the party — Marybeth's food, Rance's outfit, the pool tournament he'd won with Clint, Beau's trash talk during the darts game, the checkers win.

Then they made love again. They weren't just having sex anymore. Maybe they never had been.

Although she'd cherished every moment of their intimate connection, his underlying distress filtered through the layers of joy. Was he just tired? She didn't buy it.

But late at night wasn't the time to delve into thorny issues. She waited until morning, after they'd taken care of the critters and settled down to breakfast. His appetite was good, so at least he wasn't sick.

After he'd eaten most of his meal and they'd chatted about the chickens and the leaning post they were going to fix, she put down her fork. "Cheyenne, is something wrong?"

He glanced up, and for a moment distress glittered in the blue depths of his eyes. Then he blinked and it was gone. "What do you mean?"

"I think something's bothering you. You seem... worried."

"I'm fine." He ate the last bites of his meal.

He wasn't fine. She knew him too well. "Okay. But if you're having a problem and it has anything to do with me, then I'd really like to know."

He swallowed the rest of his coffee and set the mug carefully on the table. "Well, there is one thing I'm concerned about."

"What?"

"You've said you're willing to expand your world and explore your options."

"Yes." Easy to say when he was her world. They would have unlimited options to explore. Together.

"You'll need space." He cleared the hoarseness from his throat. "I promise you'll have all the space you need." The words came quickly, now, as if he didn't want to linger over them. "It's important to me that you don't have any... that you don't worry about me." He took a breath. "I'll be fine."

Ah. He was still pushing the idea of her dating other guys. Her plan to gradually make him forget that scheme with good food and good loving wasn't working.

He clearly thought it would benefit her to end their relationship and enjoy the single life. Like Angie was doing. But he didn't sound happy about it.

That was encouraging. On the other hand, Angie and his mom had warned her that he'd sacrifice his own needs for what he perceived as the right thing for someone else.

Was it time to tell him he was the only man she'd ever wanted or ever would want? That they should just cut to the chase and start building a life together?

She hesitated. Every hour they spent in each other's company brought them closer and strengthened her case for bypassing the stupid experimental phase he was so stuck on. Unfortunately, ever hour was also stressing him out.

She was looking for a tipping point, the moment when he was so in love with her that he couldn't imagine her with anyone but him. He wasn't there yet. He would be. Eventually he'd come around.

Reaching across the table, she squeezed his hand. "I promise I won't worry about you." She slid her other hand under the table and crossed her fingers.

"Good news." He didn't look like it was good news. He looked like someone had just made a joke about his dead rabbit.

She loved him so much, and she couldn't say it. Not yet. Instead she gave his hand another squeeze. "Enough serious talk. It's a beautiful day to reset a fence post. Let's get to it."

He brightened. "I'll feel a lot better about putting Mischief and Mayhem in the pasture once that post isn't wobbly."

"Me, too."

He pushed back his chair. "And we're going to the Buffalo for dinner, right?"

"I'm counting on it." Another dream come true, dancing with Cheyenne at the Fluffy Buffalo.

"Great. I'm looking forward to it, too."

* * *

A day working around her ranch had obviously lifted Cheyenne's spirits. He handed her into his freshly washed black truck with a flourish. "You look amazing."

"Thanks, so do you." His blue plaid shirt brought out the blue in his eyes. Some might say it was a little tight. She would disagree.

He swung into the driver's seat, bringing with him the aroma of his pine-scented cologne. "You smell good."

"I was about to say the same to you." He buckled up and switched on the engine. "Like sugar cookies." Backing out, he pointed the truck toward town. "I still haven't figured out if you're wearing perfume or if it's your shampoo."

"It's the shampoo. Since it has a scent, why bother with perfume?"

"Smart."

"I like the way it smells, too. The label says cotton candy, but to me it's sugar cookies."

"Whatever it's called, I like it. Noticed it right away on the drive home from the Buffalo."

"I noticed your pine-scented cologne, too. I guess it makes more of an impression in an enclosed space."

"Yes, ma'am."

"You always smell good to me, though. With or without the cologne. That's another way I can tell the difference between you and Clint."

He gave her a startled glance. "You're kidding."

"Nope. I could tell you two apart blindfolded."

"That's hard to believe, Sunshine."

"You don't have to believe me, but it's true. Your scent is there right now, blended in with the pine. Makes me feel warm and cozy."

"Hm." He tapped on the steering wheel with his thumb, his expression thoughtful. "You're not just sugar cookies, either. There's something more, a scent that's just you."

"Could you find me blindfolded?"

"I think I could. Never considered the idea before. Last night I located you by listening for your voice, and your laugh."

She smiled. "Because you sure as heck can't see me when I'm surrounded by your tall family."

"You could start wearing a tall hat with blinking lights on top."

"Don't tell Angie. She'd get me one."

He chuckled. "She would." Then he fell silent and tapped on the wheel some more. "I'm glad you two are such good friends. She'll be a huge help."

She didn't have to ask what he meant. "I have a favor to ask."

"Name it."

"Could we agree not to talk about that tonight?"

He glanced at her, his expression hard to read. "Sure."

"Thanks." She searched for a topic to throw in its place. "Are you hoping for some Garth Brooks tunes tonight?"

His shoulders relaxed. "I'm always hoping for some Garth Brooks tunes. How about you? What tunes would you like to hear?"

"Any of Carrie Underwood's songs work for me."

"Got a favorite?"

"Currently it's *End Up with You*, but I've had plenty of favorites over the years." She was taking a chance telling him about this one, though.

"I'm sure I've heard it, but I can't remember how it goes."

"It's fun to dance to."

"Then let's request it."

Evidently the title hadn't alarmed him. The lyrics might, if he listened to them. "Do you pay attention to the words of a song? Or just enjoy the music?"

"Both. Unless the words are either monotonous or make no sense. But if someone took the time to carefully choose words that have meaning or tell a story, I respect that effort. I listen."

Yeah, just one more reason to be in love with Cheyenne McLintock.

"Like *Friends in Low Places*." He smiled. "I was five the first time I heard it. I had no idea what a black-tie affair was. But I understood enough to know it was my kind of story, a down-home cowboy who wasn't intimidated by some fancy dude. I'd go around singing it at the top of my lungs."

"Do you still? Because I've never heard you—"

"What's cute when you're five isn't quite so cute when you're thirty."

"I disagree. I want to hear you sing it."

He laughed. "No, you don't."

"I do, and I'm going to talk you into it. Wait and see."

"I don't think so."

"I'll sing it with you. Would that help?"

"No, ma'am. But feel free to go ahead on your own. Sing away."

"Not unless you'll do it with me. C'mon, Cheyenne, please. I know you remember the words since you loved them so much."

"Give it up, Sunshine. I think we established last Friday that I'm not a natural performer."

"You were when you were five."

"That's debatable. My mom didn't rush me down to the talent agency and announce she'd discovered a musical prodigy. She didn't ask me to perform for her friends." He grinned. "That was my idea."

"You put on a show for her friends? That's adorable! Did she take a video?"

"If she did, we don't have the equipment to play it anymore." He pulled into a parking spot in front of the Buffalo.

"I'm going to request that one tonight. It's great for line-dancing."

"If I line-dance it with you, will you stop pestering me to sing it?"

"No." She flashed him a smile. "But I won't bring it up again until we get home."

27

After being greeted by the recorded *Welcooome to the Buffaaalooo* that issued from the life-sized wooden buffalo at the entrance, Cheyenne surveyed the crowd inside and dipped his head in Kendall's direction. "Anybody here you need to say hello to?"

"Not really." She waved to a couple sitting at a far table. "Work buddies of my dad's are here, but they're not close friends of mine. How about you? Anybody you need to schmooze with?"

"No, ma'am. Discounting the two jokers behind the bar."

She glanced over and gave Clint and Rance a wave, too. "Clint must be filling in for somebody. I hardly ever see him behind the bar since his promotion."

"I'm sure he's enjoying himself. He likes being the manager, but bartending's his first love."

Cecily, the blonde forty-something hostess who had worked at the Buffalo ever since Cheyenne became old enough to drink, approached with menus. "Hey, you two. I have tables by the dance floor if you're interested."

"We'll take one, Cecily. Thanks."

"Anyone joining you?"

"Don't think so." Which had been part of his plan, to come on a night when friends and family weren't likely to show up.

"Then I'll give you a two-top." Cecily led them to a table and waited while he pulled out Kendall's chair for her and took a seat himself. She started to hand them menus and hesitated. "Do you even need these?"

"I don't, but—" He glanced across the table. "Want a menu?"

"Not unless it's changed in the past two weeks."

"It has not."

"Then I don't need to look at it, either, thanks."

"Ready to order, then?"

"I am." Kendall spoke right up. "Could I please have a barbeque sandwich with fries?"

Cecily smiled. "The usual, then. What do you want to drink?"

"Do you have any more of that local beer from Eagles Nest? I had some last time, but I can't remember the name."

"McGavin's pale ale, and yes, we have it. Got a shipment yesterday."

"Then I'd love a bottle of that, please." She glanced across the table. "If you haven't had it, I recommend giving it a try."

"That's good enough for me." He looked up at Cecily. "I'll have what she's having."

"Including the barbeque and fries?"

"Everything."

"It should come up fast, then. See you in a few." She whisked away.

Once she was gone, he leaned across the table. "I was prepared to buy you a steak dinner."

"Thank you for that, but this is the best choice if you want to dance."

"Why?"

"Lucky and I figured it out years ago. A steak dinner is too complicated."

"Seems simple enough to me."

"It is if you come to eat steak and don't care about dancing. With steak, you need to watch for it to come out. You can't keep dancing and let an expensive dinner just sit there. With barbeque and fries, it doesn't matter so much."

"Never thought of it that way."

"Makes sense, though, right? Barbeque and fries are good at any temperature. You can leave in the middle of your meal if a song comes up you love."

"You sold me. Ready to get out there?"

She beamed at him. "Can't wait. This one's good for a two-step."

"Let's go." No wonder Kendall and Lucky always looked like they were having a blast when they came here to dance. They made dancing a priority. No woman he'd brought to the Buffalo had done that.

At the edge of the floor, he whirled Kendall into his arms and slid in between two couples as they passed by. Effortless. Dancing with her shouldn't be this easy.

It wasn't just easy. It was magic. Likely her graceful moves had been honed by all those times she and Lucky had come here. Maybe she had a talent for making everyone she partnered with feel like they were born to it.

Safe to say he'd never enjoyed a dance more or regretted the end as much. Adrenaline pumping through him, he gazed at her. "I've never danced with anyone like you."

Her color was high and her breathing rapid. "That's logical. Nobody dances the same and you've never danced with me."

"It's not just that. You bring something special, maybe because you like it so much. Lucky's mentioned that you were good at this, but I had no idea—"

"Cheyenne, I've seen you out on the floor plenty of times. You're a wonderful dancer. But you've never had the right partner."

"Evidently not." The band started the next tune, a slow one, and he drew her close without bothering to glance at their table. If the food had arrived, he didn't care. Unless she wasn't into slow dancing. "You okay with staying out for another one?"

"Of course." She nestled against him and lifted her face to his. "Different mood."

He smiled. "Not as much dancing required."

"Oh, it's dancing, all right. Just very subtle."

"I'm fine with subtle." Just so he could keep holding her and moving to the music.

"Good lyrics, too."

"Mm." He wrapped both arms around her. Swaying to the gentle rhythm and holding her warm gaze, he paid attention to the words since she liked them. The tune was *When You Say Nothing at All*.

He'd heard it before, usually this version sung by Allison Krause with the late Keith Whitley dubbed in. A tender song, but not the kind he favored... or was it? He dragged in a breath. Okay, it was getting to him.

Kendall's luminous expression was so... how to describe it? More than beautiful. Incandescent. Radiant. He could look at her forever. Until the end of time. Until they were both old and feeble.

Except that wasn't how this would go. Emotions he had to stuff down made his chest ache. He swallowed what he'd promised himself not to say and closed his eyes, just for a second, so he could gather his forces.

With a sigh she laid her cheek against his chest. Opening his eyes, he leaned down and dropped a soft kiss on her freshly washed curls, breathing in the scent of sugar cookies. Not sure why he'd done that. Asking forgiveness, maybe? She hugged him tighter.

Well, this was a hell of a mess. For years he'd searched in confusion and frustration, not even sure what he was looking for. He was sure, now. Yeah, he was toast.

_28_

She'd done it. Every time Kendall looked into Cheyenne's blue eyes during the most amazing evening ever, his gaze was filled with love. He was crazy about her.

He hadn't told her, yet, but he didn't have to. Love was sticking out all over him. He was likely waiting until they got home to break the news.

Although he ate his barbeque and fries, it took a while because he kept interrupting their meal and asking her to dance. He couldn't get enough dancing, whether they were twirling around the floor to a fast number or getting cozy with a slow number where they barely moved.

As promised, he requested _Friends in Low Places_. How he got through the line dance without stepping on someone was a miracle, since he couldn't stop looking at her.

He also requested _End Up with You_, and as they two-stepped to the bouncy tune, she debated which would be their song, this one or _When You Say Nothing at All_. Maybe the slow one, since that was when he'd fallen totally in love with her.

His stunned expression when the truth had dawned would stay with her forever. He'd scared himself, so he'd had to close his eyes and get a grip. But all his actions since had confirmed the seismic shift in his thinking.

Oh, the lovemaking they'd have tonight! When he finally suggested leaving, she was only too ready. He wouldn't tell her while he was driving. Not romantic enough. He'd want to hold her and kiss her after making that declaration.

Anticipation made her antsy and the drive back to her place took eons. He wasn't the least bit chatty. She tried to make small talk about the talented vocalists who'd done such a good job tonight, especially with that Keith Whitley/Allison Krause duet. His answers were short, his focus on the road.

She understood. Telling someone you love them and want to spend the rest of your life with them... that was a big deal. She'd make it easy on him, though. Her enthusiasm and love would sweep away any misgivings left over from his previous dopey thinking that she needed to date other guys.

Loving her the way he did, he wouldn't be able to stand that idea anymore. Hallelujah. She'd waited for the tipping point and had found it on the dance floor.

When he parked in front of her house, she forced herself to stay put while he came around to help her out. He kept hold of her hand as he shut the door and started toward the front porch.

She gave his hand a squeeze. "What a fabulous night at the Buffalo. I can't thank you enough."

"It was very special." His voice sounded a little froggy.

"Sure was." Poor guy, he was overcome with the emotion of the moment. They needed to get through this part quickly so they could celebrate in bed.

Clearly he was of the same mind, because he wasted no time getting them into the house. He paused just inside the door. "Kendall, there's something I need to tell you."

"I can guess what it is." Her voice quivered with eagerness.

"I'm sure you can." He let go of her hand and faced her, his expression serious. "It must be obvious to someone as perceptive as you."

"Thank you. And I perceive that we should take off our coats." How adorable that he was too flustered to think of such things.

"I love you."

"I know! And it's the most wonderful news in the wor—"

"In some ways, you're right." He held her gaze. "I've been waiting a long time to feel like this. Thank you for showing me it's possible."

She peered at him in confusion. "What do you mean, *in some ways*? You love me, which is the best news ever, because I've loved you for a very long time. Now we can—"

"No, Sunshine. No, sweet lady. I'm selfish, but not that selfish. I love you, and because I love you, I'm backing away."

"Backing *away*?" She stared at him. "Are you out of your ever-loving mind?"

"Probably, but the sane part of me knows this is for the—"

"For the best?" Anger and disbelief left her shaking. "How can you say that? How can you possibly—"

"Because you can't know if I'm right for you! Not when I'm the only—"

"Bullshit!"

"Listen, you need—"

"No, *you* listen, Cheyenne McLintock!" She jabbed a finger into his chest. "Some people take years to figure out who's right for them. You're one of those people. Others know it from the get-go." She pointed to herself. "I'm one of those people. Don't judge me by your standards, dammit."

He flinched. "They're not just my standards. Nobody I know thinks like that."

"Nobody but *me*, hotshot. Are you saying I'm nobody?"

"Of course not. But your conclusions are based on... inadequate information."

"Let me get this straight. If I hop into bed with a bunch of different guys and still prefer you, you'll deem me ready to make that choice?"

"The way you say it sounds ridiculous, but—"

"Is it so difficult to believe that my instincts are right? That I made the perfect choice early on?"

"Hardly anybody does that, Sunshine."

"I did."

"What if you're wrong? What if we get married and a few years down the line you start wondering what you missed out on?"

"What if I'm right and you throw away a chance for something amazing because you're a coward?"

His head snapped back. "A *coward*?"

"That's what I said. I didn't peg you for one, but maybe this isn't all about me making a mistake out of ignorance. Maybe it's also that you're afraid you're not as amazing as I say you are."

"I guarantee I'm not."

She stepped closer and grabbed the lapel of his jacket. "I guarantee you are, buster. I know you. I've watched you grow into an incredible human being. Because I know you front to back, top to bottom, warts and all, I'm a better bet than any other woman you'll ever meet."

He gazed down at her, a flicker of hope in his eyes. Then it disappeared. "I'm sure you're right. You're my best bet, but—"

"Then take me! Sweep me off my feet!"

He stared at her, agony in his eyes. Then his jaw clenched and he shook his head. Gently removing her hand from his jacket, he backed away. "I'll get my things."

"I can't believe you're doing this."

"It's how I pictured it all along. Just came sooner than I thought." He started down the hall. "I'll only be a minute."

Should she follow him? Argue her case some more? No. She'd only be repeating the points she'd already made. She fought the despair that threatened to bring her to tears. She would *not* cry, at least not when he was still here.

He came back quickly, his duffle lumpy with all he'd hastily shoved into it. He paused. "I hate upsetting you."

"I hate it, too."

"But one day you'll—"

"Thank you for this? Fat chance. When did you decide to dump me?"

"I'm not dumping you. I'm—"

"When?"

"During the first slow dance."

"Then why did we stay there for hours?"

"Selfishness."

She groaned. "You're such an idiot."

"Agreed."

"I'll say it once more, in hopes it'll penetrate eventually. We're a perfect match. I've known that for a long time. In your heart, you know it, too. This self-sacrificing gesture of yours is the dumbest thing you've ever done."

"I realize you're angry, but—"

"Angry, disappointed, sick to my stomach. All of it." She glared at him.

"I need to know one thing. Were you saving yourself for me?"

She should lie. The truth wouldn't help her cause. But she couldn't do it. "Yes."

"I was afraid of that."

"You may think this is over, but it's not."

"Yes, ma'am, it is." He touched the brim of his hat. "Goodbye, Sunshine."

How dare he use her nickname as he was going out the door? If she'd had an object handy, she would have thrown it at him.

But she was empty-handed. Empty-hearted, too. No, that wasn't right. Love for him, stupid dork that he was, still swelled in her chest. He was her destiny, her soul mate, but that didn't mean he didn't have a few flaws. Or that she didn't want to smack him.

She'd have to work around his blind spots. And she'd need help.

Picking up her phone, she glanced at the clock. Too late to call. She texted instead.

Angie replied immediately. *What's up? Rance said you guys were at the Buffalo tonight.*

Kendall had held it together so far, but the instant reply from her best friend set off the waterworks. *We had an awesome time. He said he loves me. Then he dumped me.*

WTF?

I know.

I'll be right over.

<u>29</u>

Cheyenne walked into his cold, lifeless house fighting a massive headache and an earworm. He could take something for the headache, but how was he supposed to get rid of the earworm? The lyrics to *When You Say Nothing at All* would be with him for the duration.

Flipping on a light, he dropped his duffle to the floor, took off his coat and shivered. He should turn on the heat. Or build a fire. He did neither.

Standing in the middle of his sterile living room, he breathed in. The air in his house didn't smell like much of anything. He hadn't cooked in his kitchen for days, hadn't built a fire since before the bachelor auction.

He'd cleaned out the ashes last week, vacuumed the floor, dusted the surfaces, scrubbed the kitchen and bathroom. The place looked like something out of a magazine. He'd been proud of it the day he'd moved in seven years ago. Still was in a detached way. Until the past few days, it had felt like home.

A truck pulled up outside. He rushed to the door and threw it open. Had she— no. Clint's truck.

His twin climbed down and closed the driver's door. "Expecting someone? Because if she's due to come over, I'll—"

"She's not."

"Then what the hell are you doing here? Run low on little raincoats?"

"I broke it off."

"I do hope we're talking about your relationship and not your—"

"For God's sake, Clint."

"It can happen. I've read about incidents where— but clearly that's not the case." He climbed the steps. "You broke up with her?"

"Had to."

"Really? From the looks of things tonight, you two were getting along like peanut butter and jelly."

"That's why I had to end it. My fault entirely. I fell for her, if you can believe it." He stepped aside. "I assume you're coming in."

"Might as well give you some company. You look about as bad as you did when Hippity died." He peered at him. "I take that back. You look worse."

"Want a beer?"

"Sure. It's cold in here. Did you turn off the heat?"

"Didn't need it on when I was staying at Kendall's."

"But now you could..." Clint's voice trailed off. "Never mind. I'll build us a fire."

"Okay." He kicked his duffle aside with the toe of his boot, tossed his jacket over the arm of the sofa and headed for the kitchen. "Want chips, too?"

"Chips would be good. Chewing jump-starts your brain and yours is flashing the low-battery light."

Cheyenne pulled an unopened bag from the cupboard. "How'd you happen to come by tonight?"

"I check out your place every night when I'm driving by and you're on duty, or in this case, staying elsewhere. Been doing it for years."

"No kidding?"

"Just part of the service."

"I didn't know that." Made his chest hurt. It was so like Clint to do something nice and say nothing about it. "Thank you."

"You're very welcome."

He snagged two beers from the door of the fridge, opened them and returned to the living room. Clint's fire looked promising.

His twin wasn't as good at fire building as he was, but he'd made a passable effort. Kendall should have a fireplace put in, now that her dad was gone. She—his stomach lurched. Kendall wasn't his business anymore.

Plopping down on the sofa, he put the unopened chips and one of the beers on the coffee table. His head still hurt, but not as bad. He swallowed a hefty amount of his beer.

Flames leapt in the fireplace. Clint replaced the screen and turned. "You forgot coasters."

"Yep, sure did."

"You don't want rings on that nice table." Clint fetched two from the kitchen, picked up his beer and used his sleeve to wipe away the moisture before setting the bottle on one of the coasters. "Aside from not wanting rings on principle, you don't want a ring to remind you of this crappy night."

"Like I'll ever forget it."

Clint sat down, ripped open the bag of chips and took out a handful. "You said you *had* to break up with her. Can you refresh my memory on that point?"

"I had to cut her loose so she's free to date."

"And she's chomping at the bit to do that?"

"She will be once she gets over being mad. She'll thank me for getting out of her way."

"But now she hates your guts?"

"I wish." He sighed. "She loves me."

"Bummer. Must be hell to be in love with someone who loves you back."

"Smartass."

"I had a realization while you and Kendall were living it up at the Buffalo. Care to hear it?"

"Do I have a choice?"

"Nope." He took a gulp of beer and put the bottle down on the coaster with a soft click. "Little Kendall isn't a kid anymore, bro. That hasn't been as obvious when she's come in with Lucky. But dancing with you tonight, she aged up considerably. She can handle you just fine."

"Just because she can handle me doesn't mean she's savvy about guys in general."

"You think you're so special? Guys are guys. You flat-out told me she isn't a shrinking violet in bed. What's dating going to give her that you haven't?"

"A basis of comparison."

"Ah." Clint smiled. "Now we get down to it. You want her to find out what a stud you are."

"No! I—"

"Don't forget this is me you're talking to."

Chugging the last of his beer, he set it carefully on the coaster. "It's not the sex. Well, maybe a little bit. Mostly it's about exploring possibilities.   Engaging   with   different personalities."

"Of the male variety, you mean."

"Yes." Resting his forearms on his thighs, he stared at the empty bottle. "She called me a coward tonight."

"Hm."

"Maybe I am. She thinks of me as some kind of superhero. I was able to meet her expectations for a few days, but..." He glanced over at his twin. "I'd never be able to maintain that. I'd screw up. She'd become disillusioned and wish she hadn't settled for the first guy she ever—"

"Seems to me the screwing up has already happened. You said she's mad."

"Furious."

"And still loves you."

"So she says."

"Oh, I would believe her if I were you. Everybody who was at the Buffalo tonight would believe her, including me."

"She's wonderful, Clint. I had no idea how wonderful until recently, and the truth is, I'm not good enough for her. She just doesn't know it because she hasn't allowed herself to—"

"Date and have sex. I'll admit she's a little skimpy in that department. But she's been hanging out with us since she was in kindergarten. We're a good-looking bunch, if I do say so. Mostly well-behaved. Charming, in fact."

"That's important why?"

"She couldn't help but gather info about the male of the species during those years. And out of that tasty crowd she picked you, right off the bat, no hesitation."

"What does a five-year-old know?"

"More than we give them credit for. And another thing. In all that time, her allegiance never changed. Didn't matter that you didn't return her affections, or that you mostly avoided her."

"You're making my case for me. She admitted tonight she hasn't had sex until now because she was saving herself for me."

"Women still do that?"

"This one did."

"That's weird. A huge compliment, but weird."

"Like I said, she's put me up on a damned pedestal."

"Are you sure you're not playing an old tape? If I'm not mistaken, she also called you a coward."

"Yes, but—"

"I agree she's crazy about you, bro. But your pedestal might be a whole lot shorter than you think."

30

Kendall brainstormed with Angie until nearly one in the morning. Talking it out with her helped her mental state, but no concrete plan emerged. She'd finally sent Angie home to sleep. They agreed to tackle the problem again when they weren't exhausted.

Kendall woke at dawn. Resisting the urge to pull the covers over her head, she climbed out of bed, got dressed, and went outside. Right after she'd finished feeding the critters, Angie called.

"My morning appointment cancelled. I'd like to come over and bring Mom and Marybeth."

"Of course. Have you eaten?"

"Just a snack so far. We can bring cinnamon rolls."

"I'll whip up an egg casserole, cut up some fruit and make coffee."

"Excellent. See you in a few."

Kendall disconnected and got busy. The sadness that had plagued her while she'd fed the chickens and the horses eased. She put the casserole in the oven, created a fruit bowl of sliced apples, bananas and grapes, made coffee and set the kitchen table. How long since she'd entertained four people here? Months, maybe years.

If last night had gone a different way, this gathering might have been focused on wedding plans. She swallowed the sudden lump in her throat. That could still happen. Just not today.

The sound of the truck brought her out on the front porch, eager to greet them. Desiree pulled in driving her Ford F-350 with the custom purple paint job. That badass truck lifted Kendall's spirits even more. When three of the best ladies in the world piled out, she smiled for the first time since Cheyenne had walked out her door.

She hurried down the steps and they enfolded her in a group hug made slightly awkward by the pan of cinnamon rolls. Stepping back, she wiped her eyes. "I'm so glad to see you guys."

"I'm so glad to visit and see your chickens!" Desiree beamed at her. "I've heard so much about Dolly, Loretta and Reba that I feel as if I know them."

"I'll take you back there. We have a few minutes before the casserole's done." It was official. She missed having company.

Leading them through the house, she set the pan of cinnamon rolls on the counter.

"I'd forgotten how much I like your place." Desiree glanced at the kitchen as she walked through. "Authentic. Smells terrific, too."

"And don't you plant a garden every summer?" Marybeth cast an approving eye over the layout of the kitchen.

"I do. I'm almost ready to put my seedlings in the ground. It's a short season, but I make the most of it."

"That's inspiring. I tried years ago and lost heart. If you'd be willing to share your methods, I'll give it another shot."

"Absolutely." She ushered them out to the back porch.

"Oh, my goodness, a glider." Desiree walked over to inspect it. "Have you always had this?"

"Since I was a kid. It's been repaired several times, but I'm glad to put the money into it."

"I would be, too." She gazed out toward the chicken yard. "You can see those beautiful hens from here. You could sit on the glider and watch them."

"Yes, you could." She avoided looking at Angie. Last night they'd rehashed the whole glider episode and the events that had followed, searching for ways to turn things around. To no avail.

"Let's go visit those ladies of yours. I'll bet we have them to thank for the casserole you made."

"We do." Good thing her chickens were superior layers. She'd been warned when she got them that they likely wouldn't lay right away. To her delight they'd gifted her with eggs from the second day and every day thereafter.

Desiree and Marybeth admired the chickens, the coop she and Angie had built and the electric fence Cheyenne had helped her set up.

Marybeth was especially entranced. "I see chickens and a garden in my future. Now that the kids are raised, I can take the time."

"Better you than me," Desiree said. "I'll cheer from the sidelines."

"We should go in. The casserole should be ready." Kendall ushered them back to her kitchen. Everyone pitched in to get breakfast on the table and in minutes they'd all taken their seats, filled their plates and poured their coffee.

"This is lovely." Desiree glanced around. "I'm glad I had a break in my schedule. Normally I'd be at my desk by now."

"Normally I'd be heading out to an appointment," Angie said. "It's the hand of Fate that left this morning free. Oh, and I brought a contract, Kendall. Look it over and make sure you're happy with the terms and compensation."

"You know I'll rubber-stamp it."

"I know, but I want to do this right. Wow, my first employee."

"I predict you'll end up with more as you grow." Desiree looked over at Kendall. "But what could be better than starting with your best friend?"

"Who is the reason we're here this morning." Angie spread her napkin in her lap and picked up her fork. "But I vote we eat first, talk later."

"I second that," Marybeth said. "It's a treat to sit down to a meal cooked by someone besides me. I also think better after I'm fed."

Kendall smiled. "Then dig in. I've been wanting to have you at my table for years after all you've taught me."

"It's been my privilege, honey." Marybeth took a bite of the casserole.

Her hum of pleasure said it all. High praise from a woman who was a genius in the kitchen. Desiree added her compliments and, as usual, Angie raved. Nice. Almost made up for the pain of Cheyenne's rejection. Almost.

With a discussion of Cheyenne postponed, Desiree asked what projects Angie had lined up for the following week. Kendall could have kissed Desiree for introducing the only topic capable of making her forget Cheyenne for a few minutes. Her new job would be a godsend in the coming days.

As everyone finished eating, Kendall refilled coffee mugs and turned to Desiree. "Brainstorming time."

"Indeed." She cleared her throat. "Cheyenne called me this morning,"

Kendall gripped the napkin in her lap. "Did he say anything about…"

"He did." Desiree met her gaze with motherly understanding and concern. "He told me he'd backed away from the relationship and it was for the best."

Angie groaned. "What a dope. Did you tell him he had his head up his—"

"It wasn't the time to confront him. He's taking Black Jack out for a long ride, which is a good coping mechanism. It would be lovely if he had an epiphany out there, but I doubt he will after the way he sounded on the phone. He's very unhappy."

"His own damned fault." Angie scowled and took a sip of her coffee. "I don't know what's up with him."

Marybeth snorted. "Sure you do. His personal happiness has never been a priority with that boy. He'll do what he thinks is right even if it kills him."

"Except it's not right," Desiree said. "He thinks he's making a noble gesture, but his reasoning is faulty and he's questioning Kendall's judgment. Which isn't respectful."

"You're so right, Mom. He needs to hear that. I wish you'd told him when he—"

"Not over the phone, sweetie. And I wouldn't put it that way, even in person. I don't want to argue with him. But I would like to give him some things to think about."

"And I would like to give him a piece of my mind." Angie exchanged a glance with Kendall. "He's my brother and I love him, but he's so bull-headed."

"Maybe not bull-headed as much as misguided." Desiree smiled at her daughter.

"I say bull-headed. You're being way nicer than I am."

"Don't worry. I'm not letting him off the hook, but timing is everything. Unfortunately, he goes back on duty in the morning. I hate to leave this hanging until he gets off on Sunday."

"We could call a family meeting tonight," Angie said. "Oh, wait. You have the Wenches."

"I do. I suppose I could cancel book club, but—"

"No, you can't," Marybeth said. "It's Cindy's birthday."

"It sure is. I don't know how I forgot that. We already have champagne chilling. Anyway, a family meeting might be a mistake. It could turn into a bunch of wrangling."

Marybeth nodded. "Some might agree with his decision."

"Very possible. What we need is..." Desiree stared into space. Then she gasped and glanced around the table. "That's the missing piece I've been looking for. Oh, this will be perfect. It's like it was foreordained. I couldn't ask for a better way to handle—"

"Mom? Care to tell us your brilliant idea?"

"You don't see it?"

Angie gave her an indulgent smile. "No, ma'am. And it doesn't seem to be written across your forehead."

"It's so obvious. He needs a different perspective from a direction he could never imagine would be helpful. But it will be. I promise you that."

"Still not getting it, Mom."

She smiled in triumph. "The solution was right in front of us. I'll invite Cheyenne to the book club meeting."

31

After a night with very little sleep, a day spent riding a feisty Black Jack for hours, and nothing to eat but canned soup and a toasted cheese, Cheyenne was in lousy shape to meet with the Wenches.

He'd shaved, showered, and put on clean clothes. That made him feel a little more like a functioning human being. But he wasn't looking forward to the evening.

He wasn't stupid. This had something to do with Kendall, or rather his decision regarding Kendall. Would she be there?

That made no sense. Kendall didn't know that his mom was a best-selling author or that the Wenches were her beta readers. Bringing Kendall into the mix would be risky.

That said, it was the only scenario that he could come up with. He could have refused to go. It wasn't like his mom could force him to attend.

But she'd asked so sweetly, with such love in her voice, that he hadn't been able to say no. Clint might have said no. Probably would have. But he wasn't Clint.

At the appointed hour, he drove up to the house and parked. The Wenches were all there. He could identify each of their vehicles as surely as he could spot those of his family members.

He loved the Wenches, who'd been part of his life ever since he could remember. He'd mourned with the rest of his family when they'd lost Mary, Jess's mom.

They all loved him back, so whatever tonight's deal was, he didn't have to worry about it. Even so, anxiety tumbled in his gut as he climbed the porch steps. They likely had questions about his decision and wanted to offer opinions, as fond aunties would do.

Except Jess wasn't a fond auntie. Beau's wife had recently been added to the team to fill her mother's empty chair. Since she was from his generation, maybe she'd understand his reasoning better than the others.

As he crossed the porch, his mom opened the door. "I was watching for you. Thank you for coming."

"This is about Kendall, isn't it?"

"Yes, son, it is." She closed the door and waited while he left his coat and hat on the rack nearby.

"I don't see what the Wenches have to do with it."

"You will."

He turned to her. "Is she here?"

"There was no reason for it." She started down the hall.

"Have you told her anything?" He fell into step beside her.

"That would be premature."

"It's a wonder she hasn't found out, living so close and being such good friends with Angie."

"She hasn't found out for the same reason no one has unless I tell them. Why would anyone think they have a best-selling writer living next door? Authors can be invisible unless they become famous like Stephen King or J.K. Rowling."

"That could happen to you some day."

"Maybe, but I hope not. I love my life the way it is."

He wished he could say the same.

"By the way, we're having champagne. I should have asked if you wanted a beer when we passed the kitchen."

"Champagne?"

"It's Cindy's birthday."

"Ah. What color's her hair tonight?"

"Since it's her birthday month, she has at least four going on. Might be five. Want a beer? You could go back and get one. I'll let them know you'll be right in."

"No, thanks. I'll handle this without booze."

"Your choice." She walked into the library. "Our guest of honor has arrived."

"Woo-hoo!" Sounded like the birthday girl.

He followed his mom in and was greeted with cheers and smiles. He grinned. Wench birthdays took celebrating to a whole new level. Literally.

During one of his mom's renovation projects, she'd asked the carpenter to build a contraption she kept in her office. For Wench birthdays, she rolled it out, locked the wheels and unfolded it to create a raised platform with steps on one side.

The birthday girl's wingback chair, in this case Cindy's blue one, was then placed on the platform. Cindy, wearing a tiara on her spiked and rainbow-colored hair, sat in regal splendor gazing down at her subjects. She held a champagne glass in one hand and a rhinestone-studded scepter in the other.

Cheyenne managed to wipe the smile off his face. "May I approach the throne, your majesty?"

"Please do, kind sir."

He walked into the circle of wingbacks plus one dining room chair. That would be his. He executed a courtly bow. "Many happy returns, Miss Cindy."

"I accept your good wishes, Cheyenne. You may take your seat, now."

"Thank you, your majesty." Turning, he walked back to the dining room chair and sat down.

He was flanked by Teresa in the orange wingback on his left and Colleen in the red one on his right. The Wenches kept their rainbow chairs in order, rotating when the occasion called for it.

That put his mom in the violet one beside Colleen. Next came Annette perched on an indigo chair, then Cindy on the platform. Jess was on

Cindy's right in her mother's green wingback and Nancy filled out the rainbow in her yellow one.

Cindy lifted her scepter. "I call this meeting to order in the name of Louis L'Amour, the patron saint of Western novels."

Everybody toasted with their champagne flutes except him. Maybe he should have fetched that beer, after all.

Cindy continued. "Tonight, we'll depart from our usual format to discuss recent actions taken by one Cheyenne McLintock."

Colleen giggled. "Is there a second one hiding in a closet?"

Cindy lifted her chin. "That's how you say it. For emphasis."

"Extraneous word," Teresa said. "Omit."

"Here we go." Nancy sighed. "Veering off the main subject into sentence structure issues. Please give me the floor, Cindy, before we end up being here all night."

"Aren't we staying all night?" Colleen looked startled. "I told George I wouldn't be back until—"

"We're staying all night," Annette said. "But Cheyenne's not. Nancy was just making a point. A good one. We need to give her the floor so we can cut to the chase."

"Mixed metaphor!" Jess called out, smiling at Cheyenne.

He took heart from that smile.

"Okay, okay." Cindy waved her scepter. "Nancy, go for it."

"Thank you." She put her champagne glass on the small table beside her and looked at him. "I was best friends with Kendall's mother."

"Honestly?"

"Since kindergarten. Ellen fell in love with Bill when they were in grade school, which turned into serious love in high school. Neither of them dated anyone else."

He blinked. "Do you think that's why Kendall—"

"I don't know. But those two were deeply in love their entire marriage and I'm convinced Bill didn't remarry because Ellen was the only one for him."

"Kendall never said anything about that. But I can see how it would influence her thinking."

"Well, she wouldn't talk about it, would she?" Jess spoke up. "That would sound lame, like she had no dreams of her own and had to repeat her parents' love story. She doesn't strike me as a mimic. She forges her own path."

"She certainly does," Nancy said. "In that way she's like Ellen. Single-minded. She followed her instincts instead of going along with the crowd and so does Kendall."

"But..." He hesitated to say it. Heck, might as well speak his mind. "That was a different time. In today's world—"

"I told you guys he'd say that." Teresa gave them all a triumphant look. "Cheyenne, you're a wonderful guy. Also, like young people in every generation, you think the way you do things is better than the way it was done before."

"Sometimes it is."

"Sometimes. But human beings are unique. You fell in love with Kendall because she's unique. Then you expect her to behave like everybody else."

That gave him pause.

"Oh, good." Colleen gave his arm a pat. "You're thinking outside the box. More accurately, outside your personal box."

It was a teasing jab. He let it pass. "I agree that she's unique. I'm just worried that when it comes to me, she's not following her instincts, she's wearing blinders."

"And that brings up the exact point I want to make." Annette dressed more conservatively and spoke in a softer voice than any of the other Wenches. "You've basically told her she doesn't know what she's doing. That's not very respectful."

Her tone might be gentle, but the words hit him hard. "I respect her." Indignation straightened his spine. "She's amazing."

"Then if she's so amazing," Annette said quietly, "why can't you believe that she knows exactly what she's doing? And that she's made the perfect choice by choosing you?"

He sucked in air.

"We took his breath away," Nancy said. "I think that's a win."

Yeah, they'd stunned him with that one. His chest was as tight as a drum and he had no comeback. He respected the hell out of Kendall. Just because he thought she'd be better off if she....

Annette's words echoed, challenging his position. He needed to get out of there. Create some space where he could breathe again. He glanced at his mom.

She gave him a slight nod.

He stood. "If you'll all excuse me, I'd like to—"

"You're excused, Cheyenne." Cindy waved her scepter. "Our best wishes go with you."

"Thank you." He left the room and lengthened his stride as he made for the front door. Grabbing his coat and hat, he carried them outside as he pounded down the steps and almost jogged on the way to his truck. They had it wrong. He loved her. He respected her. He absolutely did, damn it!

* * *

Annette's words haunted him through two days and nights of non-stop activity at the station. The calls ran the gamut — a house fire, a wreck where one of the vehicles ignited, an older gentleman who accidentally set his front yard on fire, and even the firefighter cliché, a cat stuck in a tree.

Although he was either in motion or passed out from exhaustion, Annette's accusation wouldn't leave him alone. Because she was right.

Which filled him with shame. He wasn't worthy of Kendall, after all. But that didn't mean he didn't want to see her more than he wanted to breathe.

Around ten on Saturday night he sent her a text. *Can I come by in the morning?*

Her reply was instantaneous. *I'll be waiting.*

Thank God. She wasn't going to deny him access just because he'd walked out on her. But maybe he should be more specific about his arrival time. He started another text when a call came in. He tucked his phone away and headed out with the crew.

_32_

In the morning. Kendall was awake at four, blaming her excitement for why she'd failed to ask Cheyenne for clarification. She had one parameter to work with. He couldn't leave until his shift ended. That was at eight.

What if he decided to go home and shower before he came by? What if he stopped for a bite in town before he drove out here?

And why was he coming to see her? Desiree had called Friday morning to report that the book club meeting clearly had made an impression on him, but she couldn't predict what he'd do next.

Was this a visit to discuss what had been said at the book club? Or something else? Yeah, she should have answered with something other than _I'll be waiting._ Something like _why are you coming and when will you be here?_

Since she hadn't done that, she might as well get up. The chickens weren't awake yet. Neither were the horses. Too early to start breakfast.

Oh, well. She could bake sugar cookies. By the time she'd refilled the cookie jar, the sun was peeking over the horizon.

She walked out into the cool morning, which felt lovely on her skin. Between baking and agitating over Cheyenne's visit, she was a hot mess.

Feeding Dolly, Loretta and Reba while singing their special song calmed her down quite a bit. Delivering hay flakes to Mischief and Mayhem helped, too. Since Cheyenne couldn't possibly arrive for another hour, maybe more, she hung around the barn watching the horses munch on their hay flakes.

When they finished, she led them out to the pasture and turned them loose. They raced around, scattering dew that sparkled in the sunlight.

She leaned against the gate that was no longer cattywampus and soaked up the energy of those two horses. Thanks to Mischief, Mayhem would never be a sedentary mare. They were good for each other. Like she and Cheyenne could be if....

No, that wasn't a helpful train of thought. Her new job. That was fertile ground. Tomorrow she'd move through her routine much faster. She and Angie had an appointment at nine with a couple who wanted their front porch repaired.

But today... today she'd allowed herself to be involved in this crazy situation where Cheyenne was *coming by* but she had no idea when or why. Next time, if there was a next time, she'd make sure to ask him what in the devil... hey, was that a rider in the distance?

He was coming from the east, with the sun behind him. She took off her hat and used it to block the light so she could see better. Yep, a rider, riding from the direction of Rowdy Ranch. Galloping. Couldn't be Angie, though. This was a black horse and Angie rode a buckskin.

Cheyenne had a black horse. She studied the rider more closely. Could be him. Odd that he'd chose to ride over here instead of driving his truck.

And yet, the gesture had a romantic vibe. She'd be wise not to put too much significance on his choice of transportation, though. On the other hand, if he wanted to stir her up, he'd chosen a good way to do it. Cheyenne McLintock mounted on Black Jack and coming in fast would turn any girl's head.

Skirting the pasture fence, he slowed to a trot and threaded his way between the fence and the barn. He walked Black Jack the rest of the way as he came toward her. "Good morning, Sunshine."

The sound of his voice added to the adrenaline pumping through her. "Good morning, Cheyenne." Her voice was shakier than she'd like it to be. "What brings you by?"

"You." He dismounted and dropped the reins to the dirt. "I assume you knew about my visit to the book club Thursday night."

"I did." His eyes were so blue. And so serious, easily as serious as when he'd told her they were finished.

"Did you hear anything about it?"

"Your mom said she couldn't predict what you would do."

"When I left, I couldn't have predicted it, either. But by last night, I knew I had to see you and apologize."

"For what?"

"Not believing you."

Her heartbeat picked up. "Oh?"

"I didn't give you credit for knowing who you are and what you need. Basically, I didn't respect you or your decision. I thought I knew better. That was arrogant. I'm sorry, Kendall."

Her heart pounded so fast she had trouble breathing. "It's okay."

"It's not okay. I said I wasn't good enough for you and my behavior only proves it."

She swallowed. "You're not perfect. I know that. Neither am I."

"Yes, you are. Perfect for me, anyway. But as for me, I'm—"

"Hang on, there, buster." She closed the space between them and grabbed a fistful of his shirt. "You're about to get in trouble again."

"I am?"

"A minute ago, you apologized for not believing that I know what I need."

"I did say that."

"I need you." She looked him in the eye. "Do you believe me?"

"I want to."

"Do you love me?"

His voice roughened. "With everything in me."

"Then believe that I love you just as much."

He shook his head. "Not possible."

"*Cheyenne*." She jerked on his shirt.

His gaze held hers and gradually the anxiety faded. The warm glow that replaced it was a beautiful sight. She let go of his shirt and cupped his face in both hands. "Do you believe me, now?"

"Yes." He wrapped her in his arms and pulled her in tight. His voice was husky. "I believe you now."

"I want to marry you."

He smiled. "You took the words right out of my mouth."

"Whoops. Sorry."

"Will you marry me, Sunshine?"

She just stood there grinning.

"What?"

"It's silly."

"Tell me anyway."

"When I fantasized this moment, you called me Kendall."

"Okay. Will you marry me, Kendall?"

"But I like it better the other way."

He laughed. "Will you marry me, Sunshine?"

"I will!"

"Thank you." Nudging back his hat, he cradled the back of her head and leaned down, his lips brushing hers. "That was way more complicated than it should have been."

"But we did it."

"Yes, ma'am." His mouth settled over hers.

His kiss was subtly different, still thorough and sexy enough to make her want to rip his clothes off, but with an underlying pledge that he wasn't going anywhere.

When she'd completely melted into him, he slowly lifted his head. "I want to live in your house."

"I'm glad, because I— wait a minute. What about your house?"

"Do you want to live in it?"

"Not if you're living in my house."

"You know what I mean."

"I'm teasing, but would you really rather live here?"

"I've felt at home in your place from the first day. I like my house, but I love this one, almost as much as I love you."

"Well, of course I'd be happy to stay here. It's home to me, too, but then yours will sit vacant, and that—"

"I have a temporary solution. A buddy from work just lost his place. His landlord is selling it to his daughter. I told him he could stay at my house for the time being, until he figures out what he wants to do."

She wound her arms around his neck and looked up into his adorable face. "You're such a poser."

"Why do you say that?"

"You start out talking like you don't deserve me and I should probably kick you to the curb. Then it turns out you've given away the keys to your house because you're planning to stay here. What if I'd said no?"

"To quote my brother, I couldn't picture you saying no, but if you had, I was prepared to beg. I can't live without you, Sunshine."

"Is that why you rode Black Jack over here? You want to stable him in my barn instead of at Rowdy Ranch?"

"Yes, ma'am. If that would work for you."

"Sure would."

"Just because I have him here doesn't mean I'll ignore Mayhem. I'll rotate between—"

"I wasn't thinking about that. I was thinking about barn sex. We never did it."

"I know. But if you're talking about now...."

"I'm not. Too complicated. Let's unsaddle Black Jack and put him in the corral. Later we'll introduce him to Mischief and Mayhem and then show him where he'll be sleeping."

He smiled. "And then what?"

"I'd like to show you where you'll be sleeping."

"I thought you might be heading in that direction."

"But first I want another one of those kisses."

"What kind is that?"

"The kind that tastes like forever."

"Coming right up." He tugged her close and captured her mouth with a soft moan of pleasure.

She kissed him back for all she was worth. Meanwhile, deep in her heart, a little five-year-old girl clapped her hands and jumped for joy. At last. Her happy-ever-after.

* * * * *

**Saddle up for
TESTING THE COWBOY'S RESOLVE,
book three in the Rowdy Ranch series!**

* * * * *

New York Times bestselling author Vicki Lewis Thompson's love affair with cowboys started with the Lone Ranger, continued through Maverick, and took a turn south of the border with Zorro. She views cowboys as the Western version of knights in shining armor, rugged men who value honor, honesty and hard work. Fortunately for her, she lives in the Arizona desert, where broad-shouldered, lean-hipped cowboys abound. Blessed with such an abundance of inspiration, she only hopes that she can do them justice.

For more information about this prolific author, visit her website and sign up for her newsletter. She loves connecting with readers.

VickiLewisThompson.com

Lightning Source UK Ltd.
Milton Keynes UK
UKHW010814210223
417382UK00006B/350